350

Step-Chain

All over the country children go to stay with step-parents, stepbrothers and stepsisters on the weekends. It's just like an endless chain. A step-chain. *One Mom Too Many* is the first link in this step-chain.

I'm Sarah, and my parents are separated. Not for much longer, if I have my way. Why should I have to stay with *her* and her "perfect" daughters whenever I want to see my dad? They're not my family, and I don't need *her*.

Collect the links in the step-chain! You never know who you'll meet on the way . . .

 1 One Mom Too Many! - Sarah

 2 You Can't Fall For Your Stepsister - Ollie

Coming Soon:

 3 She's No Angel - Lissie

 4 Too Good To Be True - Becca

 5 Get Me Out Of Here - Ed

 6 Parents Behaving Badly - Hannah

Step-Chain

ONE MOM TOO MANY!

Ann Bryant

Lobster Press ™

One Mom Too Many!
© 2001 Series conceived and created by Ann Bryant
© 2001 Cover illustration by Mark Oliver

Published in Canada by:
Lobster Press™
1620 Sherbrooke Street West, Suites C & D
Montréal, Québec   H3H 1C9
Tel. (514) 904-1100 • Fax (514) 904-1101 • www.lobsterpress.com

Publisher: Alison Fripp
Graphic Production: Tammy Desnoyers

Distributed in the United States by:
Publishers Group West
1700 Fourth Street
Berkeley, CA 94710
1-800-788-3123

First published in Great Britain in 2001 by Mammoth,
an imprint of Egmont Children's Books Limited, London

National Library of Canada Cataloguing in Publication

Bryant, Ann
      One mom too many! / Ann Bryant.

(Step-chain series v. 1)
ISBN 1-894222-78-4

      I. Title. II. Series.

PZ7.B873On 2003   j823'.92   C2003-902311-7

Printed and bound in Canada.

CONTENTS

Step-Chain

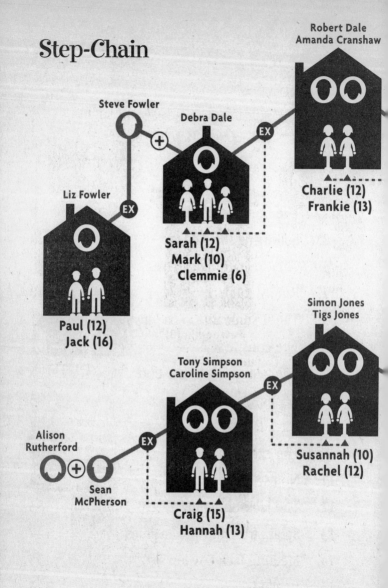

Robert Dale
Amanda Cranshaw

Steve Fowler

Debra Dale

EX

Charlie (12)
Frankie (13)

Liz Fowler

EX

Sarah (12)
Mark (10)
Clemmie (6)

Paul (12)
Jack (16)

Simon Jones
Tigs Jones

Tony Simpson
Caroline Simpson

EX

Alison
Rutherford

EX

Susannah (10)
Rachel (12)

Sean
McPherson

Craig (15)
Hannah (13)

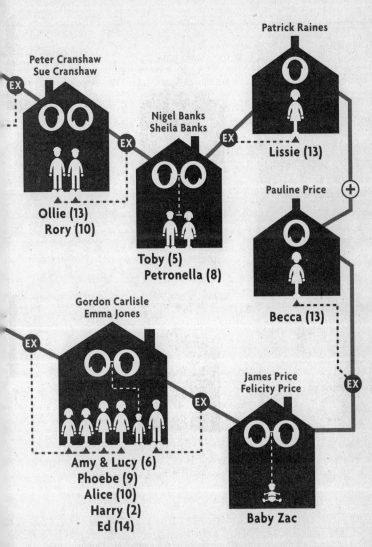

Read on to discover all the links . . .

1. THE HOME-WRECKER

It's indoor recess at school and I'm sitting at my desk reading while the rest of the class tries to break the sound barrier. It's not that I'm a goody-goody, I'm just totally teed off. Uh-oh! Teacher alert!

"Why can't you all follow Sarah Dale's example and sit down quietly with a book?"

Of course, the noise level went straight back up again the moment the teacher left the room, but a few of my friends must have suddenly realized that I wasn't joining in with their game of *Pick-the-pencil-case-up-off-the-floor-with-your-teeth*. They gathered round my desk, wanting to know what was up with me.

"You never sit and read during recess. What's the matter?' said Kelly.

"*Her.*" I couldn't be bothered to say any more. I was just too annoyed.

"Who?" asked Katie.

"You know, Sarah's . . ." Holly began.

"Don't say the word *stepmother*, or I'll kill you," I warned Kelly.

"I wasn't going to say . . . that. I was going to say 'Sarah's dad's . . .'" Holly tried again.

"Don't say girlfriend or – "

"I think I'd better shut up. My life's at risk here," said Holly. She was smiling, but then she could afford to smile. Her mom and dad still lived under the same roof.

"What's her name, your dad's . . . er . . . friend?" asked Kelly.

"I'm not saying it. I've made a vow to myself that her name will never pass my lips. She's a home-wrecker."

"Here, write it down," said Katie, passing me a scrap of paper and a pen.

I wrote *Amanda* and they all stared at it, but thank goodness no one said it out loud.

"That's the name of our neighbor's budgie," Lauren informed us seriously, and we all cracked up laughing. Even me.

Lauren is my best friend, and she already knew *her* name, but she hadn't spread it round because she's such a sweet, kind person. She probably made it up about her neighbor's budgie, because she could tell I was getting upset. She was right. It was a huge relief when the bell went.

Last night, on the phone, Dad gave me the wonderful (ha ha!) news that from now on, starting this weekend, we will be spending every other weekend with him. Up till that point in the conversation I felt fine. It was the next bit that nearly made me rush to the bathroom and want to be sick. In order to see our father, we will have to stay in *her* house! The thought of doing that every other weekend is too much to bear. I really don't see why Dad can't come home for just two days out of fourteen. It's not asking much, is it?

I asked if *her* children would be there, and he said it had been specially organized so that they would be, because *she* thought it would be more fun for us three to have some other children around. Apparently *her* children have been visiting their own father on alternate weekends for nearly a year now. Dad went on to tell me — in this wonderful phone call of his — that, what's more, the girls positively love the arrangement. They tell all their friends that they have two of everything — two homes, two birthdays, two Christmases . . . Dad made it sound like something everybody ought to be doing. I couldn't stand the way he went on and on about it, because it was obvious he was just digging around for ways of making an awful situation seem half bearable.

"Just tell me one thing, Dad," I'd interrupted him.

"Fire away," he'd said.

"What makes you assume that out of all the millions of children in the world, I would particularly pick *her* two to spend a whole weekend with?"

I could practically *hear* Dad's brain ticking over, trying to find an answer to that one. Eventually he said, "Well, what makes you think that out of all the millions of children in the world, you're *not* going to like Amanda's two?"

"I would have thought that was obvious."

There was a pause, then Dad coughed and went for a nice confident tone of voice.

"Everything'll turn out fine, Sarah. You'll see."

"What? For you, you mean?"

"No, I meant for you," he replied. Then his voice softened. "I only care about your happiness, you know," he added.

Which was a big mistake. I could have gone on for ages about how he should have thought about that when he left us. But I've said it all before, so I just kept silent. Dad then stumbled on about little bits of news that didn't interest me in the slightest, because they all contained the name of the home-wrecker.

Finally he asked to speak to Clemmie or Mark. As I handed the phone to Mark, I told him, without covering the mouthpiece, that he was in for a great weekend with four girls. Then I went off to ask Mom why this new arrangement had been made behind my back.

"Please don't harass me, Sarah," said Mom. "It hasn't been easy for me either, you know. I've got to get used to the idea of your having a sort of . . . well, a sort of stepmother, I suppose."

"They haven't gone and got married without telling us, have they?" I said, knowing that I was sounding shrill and childish but not being able to help it.

"No, no. Nothing like that. I just don't know what else to call her," Mom said, frowning at the kitchen table as though the answer might be chiseled into it somewhere.

"I do," I told her flatly. "The home-wrecker."

Mom put her arm round my shoulders and didn't speak for a moment. Neither did I, because I was getting over the horrible shock of thinking they might have gone and got married. All the time they lived together, without actually getting married, there was a greater chance that they might realize the whole thing had been a terrible mistake and go back to their proper partners. Well, Dad might anyway. I didn't care about *her*.

She could rot in hell as far as I was concerned.

Mom was still staring at the kitchen table. She looked sad. It suddenly occurred to me that she might be worried in case we three ended up liking *her* better than Mom.

"I'm never going to use the word 'stepmother,' you know. I only need one mother, and that's you."

Mom smiled at me. She was trying to be brave.

"You may find that you like her without even meaning to, you know," she said.

"No chance," I told her darkly.

"You don't have to think of her as a stepmother. Just try and like her enough to . . ."

"Enough to what? To put up with being in her company for two out of every fourteen days?" I interrupted.

"No, a bit more than that," laughed Mom.

I didn't want to get angry with Mom because

nothing was her fault. All the same, she needed to be set straight about a thing or two.

"I do have my own life to lead with my friends, you know. It'll completely ruin it if I have to go and stay miles away every two weeks. Have you thought about that?"

"Let's just take one step at a time, Sarah. See how you get along this weekend for a start."

So after that phone call last night, I had four days to think what to do. These were the options:

1. Go along with it.
2. Refuse to go.
3. Get one of my friends to smuggle me into their house for the weekend without Mom or Dad knowing.

I decided it might be best to keep the third option in reserve for a later date. The second option was still my favorite, but only just. Ninety-nine per cent of me didn't want to have anything to do with the home-wrecker, but – and I hated to admit this – one per cent of me was eaten up with curiosity. I badly wanted to see what kind of person had taken my dad away from his family. I hoped she was really hideous looking. But then Dad wouldn't have chosen someone who looked hideous, would he? It was bad enough thinking of Dad with a beautiful woman, but an ugly one would be far worse. On the other hand, if she was really ugly there was more chance of Dad dumping her and coming back to Mom.

My mind was doing somersaults trying to work everything out. I wished there was a simple solution – some kind of sign that would tell me what was going to happen. All I wanted to know was whether there was any chance of Dad coming back to Mom. I shut my eyes to think better.

Millions of pictures of *her* whizzed in and out of focus, and the tighter I squeezed my eyelids the faster they came and went. Was she tall or small or medium? Medium. Yes, definitely medium. Was she blond, dark or mousy? Um . . . blond, I guessed. Brown eyes, blue eyes, green eyes, hazel eyes? Probably blue or bluey gray. Short hair or long hair? I couldn't decide. I could picture her easily with both short hair *and* long.

I opened my eyes wide and held my breath. This must be the sign. Everything else had been easy to picture. She was medium height with blond hair and blue eyes, but I'd no idea how long her hair was. Closing my eyes again and breathing deeply, I told myself exactly what the sign meant. If it turned out that she had long hair, it meant that Dad would leave her and come back to Mom. If her hair was short, it meant that Dad and she would stay together.

From that moment on I became obsessed with the length of *her* hair.

2. FOLLOWING THE SIGN

For ages now, Dad's wanted me to meet the woman who's broken up our family, but I've simply refused every time he's mentioned it. So he's got into the habit of coming round to see us at our house. I won't even phone him at *her* house, because it would be unbearable if she or one of her daughters answered. I mean, how can it be fair that Dad's living with them and not us?

"What do *you* think about the idea of meeting Amanda and Charlie and Frankie?" Dad had asked Mark once.

"Don't mind," Mark mumbled. "Yeah . . . if you want."

Mark knew that I was dead against meeting her, so he was always careful not to sound too enthusiastic when I was around. I wondered whether he reacted completely differently when I wasn't there. I doubted it. And now the dreaded time had come I couldn't exactly imagine my nice, quiet, down-to-earth brother saying, "Oh wow! Yea-eah! Bring on the week-end!"

On Wednesday evening Dad came around because Mom wanted to talk to him about a bill. He'd never been over on a Wednesday before. It must be all part of my new-found sign. Here was the perfect opportunity to ask about the length of *her* hair. All I needed was an opening. And what do you know? Clemmie, my cute and crazy six-year-old sister, came up with the goods in true Clemmie fashion!

"When are we seeing Amanda the panda?" she asked Dad.

(She'd been doing poetry at school. It had obviously made an impression!)

"On Friday after school," Dad replied.

I took a deep breath and asked him the million-dollar question as casually as I possibly could.

"What does she look like?"

His face lit up, as though I'd offered to be a bridesmaid or something.

"Oh, you two have to meet one another. I just know you'll really hit it off."

"Look, Dad, I don't want to meet her. Not ever. I was only asking what she looked like. I'm not really all that interested even. I was just making polite conversation."

Even as I spoke, I was feeling cross with myself. I didn't like sounding so irate every time I opened my mouth to speak to Dad, but I simply couldn't help it. He didn't bat an eye, just launched straight into a description. I pretended to be far more interested in my nails, but really I was all ears.

"Well, she's quite small . . . and slim . . . with blue eyes and fair hair."

Yeah, go on, Dad. Go on! I couldn't believe that he'd stopped when it was just getting interesting. I'd got the blue eyes and the fair hair right, but I was desperate to know how long her hair was. I could hardly ask though, after I'd been so quick to tell him that I wasn't really interested.

"Can you give Dad and me five minutes, Sarah?' Mom interrupted. "Clemmie can watch the end of the video that's in the VCR."

So I took Clemmie out, and a plan began to form in my mind. I would get Clemmie to find out about *her* hair, and while she was at it, she could ask all the other things I wanted to know about, like what kind of clothes she wore and how old she was. But it had to be subtle. I didn't want Clemmie saying, "Dad, Sarah wants to know what Amanda's hair looks like."

So I drew a picture of a woman with very short, extremely curly yellow hair and blue eyes. I cunningly made sure that no other features particularly stood out, then I dressed the woman in black trousers, a black jacket and big dangly earrings.

"I wonder if Dad's friend looks like this?" I asked Clemmie casually.

"Do you mean Amanda?"

I nodded.

She studied my wonderful art and, right on cue, came out with the very words I wanted to hear, "Let's ask him."

Dad was standing by the kitchen table studying the bill while Mom stood by the stove with her arms folded. I only hoped the five minutes was up, because Clemmie went crashing in, the words tumbling out of her mouth, while I strolled in behind her, the drawing stuffed in my jeans pocket.

"What does Amanda look like, Daddy? Does she ride a motorbike?"

I closed my eyes in despair of the girl. The black clothes on my drawing had obviously conjured up completely the wrong image.

"Amanda? No, no. Just a boring old car, I'm afraid."

"Is it a green car?"

"No, it's —"

"A black car?"

"No . . ."

I needed to get Clemmie back on course before she reeled off every color known to man. Fortunately, Mom was bending down getting something out of a cupboard, and Dad's eyes were back on the bill.

I pulled the drawing out of my jeans pocket and flashed it at Clemmie.

"Is she the fairest lady in the land, Dad?"

"Er . . . no, probably not the very fairest," answered Dad absent-mindedly.

"But does she keep asking the mirror on the wall if she's the fairest of them all?"

I coughed and frowned but Clemmie didn't get the message.

Somewhere along the line, somebody must have said the word "stepmother" in her hearing, and all she could think of now was Snow White. So that was the end of my little scheme and since Mark would never take an interest in anything to do with women's looks, I had no choice but to find out for myself.

The decision was made. I would meet the home-wrecker, her two daughters, Charlie and Frankie, and their Lab, Rosie (what a stupid girlie name for a dog!). But if the adults thought for one moment that they'd got their own way, they had another think coming!

3. THE DREADED DAY ARRIVES

All through school on Friday my mind was on the approaching weekend from hell.

"Getting excited about meeting your dad's girlfriend, Sarah?" asked Tom Broom, with a silly grin on his face.

"Shut up, big ears," said Lauren, putting her arm round me and steering me away from the class eavesdropper. "Don't listen to him, Sare. Just get through the weekend somehow, and then come and tell us all about it on Monday. It'll probably turn out tons better than you think it's going to be."

"I bet Clemmie's looking forward to it, isn't she?" asked Katie.

"Yeah, she's acting totally over the top. It gets on your nerves."

I rolled my eyes, but inside I was dreading the thought of Clemmie and *her* hitting it off really well. I didn't want any of us to like her. I wanted the weekend to be a total disaster as far as *she* was concerned. That would pay her back about one per cent for all that she'd done to us. The other ninety-nine per cent payback would follow later.

It was six o'clock when Dad arrived to collect us. I'd been looking out of my bedroom window because I wanted to be forewarned if *she* was with him in the car. As the car rolled up my heart started to thump.

Don't let her be there. Don't let her be there.

I strained to see. The car stopped. Was she? Was she? No! Good. Then I saw Dad look in the car mirror and kind of smooth his hair back before he got out. I felt an instant little thrill of hope. He cares what he looks like. It can't be for our benefit. He must want to look nice for Mom.

Maybe, just maybe, he still likes her and he regrets leaving her. Perhaps the awful nightmare we've been living through is almost over. Yes, that's it! He's changed his mind. It's not too late. Mom hasn't got anyone else. She's sure to forgive him and everything will be back to normal.

I skipped downstairs and opened the front door before Dad had even rung the bell. He looked surprised but very pleased to see my smiling face. I called out to Mom.

"Dad's here, Mom!'

She came to the door with a suspicious look on her face. Dad immediately looked wary. I read what was going on in a flash. Dad thought I was smiling because I wasn't coming after all. He thought I'd got Mom to break the news. Mom thought I'd called her because Dad had said something to make me change my mind about going. The two of them were watching each other like a pair of cats, each waiting for the other to make a move. Mom recovered first.

"I think I'll check that Clemmie hasn't re-packed her bag," she said, rolling her eyes at me, because we both knew that Clemmie had re-packed five times in the last half-hour.

Dad hugged me awkwardly and told me my pants looked nice. Great! I thought. Mom and Dad aren't getting back together, any more than the moon is dripping gold coins on to our doorstep. But hey! Who cares! Dad likes my pants!

On the way to *her* house, Clemmie was acting like we were off to Disney World or something. She was on one big high and wouldn't get off it. Mark was silent. I think he was feeling quite anxious about staying somewhere completely new and strange. But it was impossible to tell what was going on in Mark's head most of the time.

Personally, I was making it absolutely clear that I had no intention of joining in the pathetic game of "One Big Happy Family". I could just imagine Dad and *her* planning it all yesterday evening.

"We'll just be completely natural . . ."

"Absolutely, because Sarah in particular is sure to have been affected by . . . you know . . . everything."

"That's right, so she'll need lots of TLC."

Tender loving care! It made me sick when people called it TLC. I bet *she* did. Actually, I *hoped* that she did, because that would make her lose even more points on my home-wreckometer.

"Here we are, then," said Dad in a very bright, isn't-this-exciting voice.

We had pulled into the drive, which was big enough for two cars. We were parked next to a red Sierra. I glanced at the license plate, hoping that it spelt COW. I got out of the car without saying anything and deliberately didn't look up at any of the windows, in case *she* was looking out. She might wave or something nauseating like that. The house looked bigger than ours.

"It's quite a big house, isn't it, Daddy?" said Clemmie.

"Call him Dad," I told her. "You grew out of calling him Daddy ages ago. What are you suddenly being all babyish for?"

I knew I shouldn't have snapped at her, and her next words made me feel really sorry for making her all confused.

"It's quite a little house, isn't it, Dad?"

"You just said it was quite big," Mark commented.

"Because it's quite big *and* quite little," said Clemmie. But she must have suddenly felt really stupid because she promptly burst into tears. Part of me wanted to cuddle her, but another part was thinking, Great! Just keep right on crying until we get inside, Clemmie, then *she'll* see how much we don't want to be here.

"Hey, what's all this?" said Dad, as he swung Clemmie up in the air and kissed the top of her head. "Actually, I quite agree and so does Amanda. Sometimes the house looks big and sometimes it looks little."

He put Clemmie down, took her hand firmly and swung her arm as he walked towards the front door. It was so false and show-offy. Mark obviously thought so too, because he caught my eye then pretended to stick his fingers down his throat to make himself sick. My feelings exactly. Good old Mark. I let a giggle escape and Dad instantly turned around.

"See, Clemms," (Dad's pet name for Clemmie), "you've made your sister giggle." And Dad chuckled too, which was even more nauseating. I just wished he'd stop trying so hard.

"I was laughing at a private joke between Mark and me," I said, making my voice sound as horrible as possible.

And then the door was suddenly opened and one of *her* daughters was standing there.

"Hi, Robert. Hi, everybody. Come in." I didn't want a complete stranger who wasn't even a grown-up calling my dad by his first name. He was my dad, not hers, and I would make absolutely sure she got that firmly into her head before this weekend was over. "I'm Charlie, by the way. I talk a lot, don't I, Robert?"

" 'Fraid so," said Dad, grinning like a Cheshire cat.

I rolled my eyes at Mark. This was unbelievable! But Mark wasn't even looking at me. His eyes seemed to be glued to Charlie. His mouth was practically dropping open. He obviously thought she looked fantastic with her long blond wavy hair and big brown eyes. I groaned inside.

"This is Clemmie," Dad was saying, as he bustled us all through the front door. I deliberately hung back and went in last because I didn't want anyone to think for a single moment that I was keen on this whole stupid weekend idea. We were standing in the hall, near the bottom of the stairs. The walls were a sort of dark orange color that looked really modern, and the carpet was very thick. It felt plusher than our house.

"Do you want to tell Charlie how old you are, Clemms? Hmm?"

Oh, why didn't he put a sock in it? It was truly unbearable.

Then the other sister appeared from one of the three rooms that led off the hall.

"This is Frankie," Charlie introduced her sister.

"Hi," said Frankie, her eyes smiling at Clemmie, who was looking from one sister to the other as though she'd just tumbled into the middle of the story of Sleeping Beauty and found herself surrounded by golden sparkling fairies. Even Mark was still gawking. I wanted to clap my hands loudly to bring them back to earth.

Charlie and Frankie looked like identical twins even though there was a year between them. Apart from the hair, which tumbled down to their waists, they were both wearing French Connection tops and Nike trainers. I just needed the wicked stepmother to turn up and my happiness would be complete.

Next thing — what do you know? — my wish (ha ha!) comes true.

"Hi . . ." she said, plunging into the middle of our family, clutching a portable phone. She was trying to reach the windowsill and I happened to be the person nearest to it. "Sorry . . . can you pass me that piece of paper please, Sarah? Yeah, that's the one . . . thanks. Sorry, I'm just on the phone. Won't be a sec . . ."

Then off she scooted. She'd hardly looked at us. I mean, she'd given me a passing smile, but I could tell she wasn't concentrating or anything. And she hadn't even looked at Clemmie or Mark. I couldn't believe it. I was really cross with myself. I'd already blown my resolution to be as uncooperative as possible, and I'd only been inside the door for about thirty seconds.

It was just that she'd caught me off guard. I hadn't known what she was talking about, and I'd passed the paper over in a sort of dream. She hadn't acted at all as I'd expected. Maybe that was all part of the plan, and she wasn't really on the phone, but she just figured that it would be the least embarrassing way to get over the initial awkwardness. Well, she needn't think she was getting off that lightly. She'd still got plenty of awkward bits to come.

4. FAMILY SOLIDARITY?

"Clemmie and Sarah are sharing with us two and Mark's got the spare room. Do you want us to show you?" said Charlie.

"Whoa, not so fast," Dad said, making his voice sound all merry and breezy. "What about coats off first, hmm?"

He might as well have been talking to himself. Clemmie and Mark (still firmly locked under the spell of the golden girls) followed the two heads of swinging blond hair upstairs. Then something beeped in the kitchen and Dad whizzed off, saying he'd better see to it as *she* was on the phone. Which left me standing there like a spare part. And that (wouldn't you just know it?) was when *she* came off the phone and found me.

"Sorry, Sarah. It was my mother." Then, practically talking to herself as she reached past me to put the piece of paper back, "She sure has a knack of choosing her moments!" She looked round in surprise. "Where is everyone?"

"Gone to look at their rooms," I mumbled.

"Do you want to go up too, or would you like a bit of peace for two minutes?"

So this was her game: treat me like a casual friend, then I couldn't accuse her of trying to take Mom's place. OK, I'd play the same game, and we'd see who won.

"I'll go up, I think."

"I'm sorry it'll be a bit squished. I was saying to your dad that it might be an idea to get some sort of partition for that room, then you'd at least get a bit of privacy."

I didn't know if she was expecting me to thank her or what, but I just turned towards the stairs. At that moment Dad appeared from the kitchen.

"The lasagna's practically done. Should we eat now, Mand?"

(Mand? Yuk!)

"Fine by me," she answered.

They were both carrying on as though I wasn't there. Where were all the brightly false embarrassing remarks? Where had Dad's forced jollity gone? Why was *she* being so incredibly *ordinary*?

A cloud of depression came over me as I slowly climbed the stairs. This wasn't how I'd thought it would be at all. I could just imagine the conversation at school on Monday.

KELLY: So what's she like, your dad's friend?

ME: Just ordinary really.

KELLY, HOLLY, KATIE AND LAUREN: Oh . . . right.

Yep, that should get them interested. Ha ha! My only consolation was that there was plenty of weekend to go, plenty of time for her and Dad to make lots of mistakes.

It was when I was almost at the top of the stairs that I suddenly remembered something – *her* hair. Was it short or was it long? I stopped in my tracks and wondered how I could possibly have overlooked this most crucial thing. Everything had been so fast, and there'd been so much going on, I just hadn't noticed.

I shut my eyes and tried to visualize her. It was long. Yes, definitely long. Well, nearly down to her shoulders. Did that count as long? It was sort of scooped under at the bottom, and I was sure it went way past her chin. Or did it? I *had* to know immediately. There was a lot hanging on the length of the home-wrecker's hair — the future of two families for a start.

The sound of laughter and happy high-pitched voices came seeping out from under the bedroom door. So they'd shut me out, had they? I could even hear Mark laughing. He was supposed to be my ally. Huh! Fat chance! I bet no one had noticed that I wasn't there. Well, let them have their fun without me. They made me sick.

I left my bag at the top of the stairs and tiptoed back down again. All I had to do was catch a glimpse of the hair, then I'd head straight back upstairs again and no one would be any the wiser. I could hear her talking in a really gooey voice. How revolting! I'd stumbled into a lovey-dovey conversation of theirs. It was odd though, because Dad wasn't saying anything. I was right outside what must have been the living-room. Through the half open door I could see a green and cream-colored sofa and the end of a dresser.

"You're such a lovely old thing, aren't you?" *she* was saying. I just prayed they weren't actually kissing, otherwise there was quite a risk that I'd anoint the hall carpet by throwing up all over it.

If I just moved a little to the left, I felt sure I'd be able to see her . . . Suddenly a boisterous great Lab came hurtling out of the door, and rushed at me excitedly. Unfortunately, it couldn't stop in time so it crashed into me, making me stumble. Trying to get my balance as quickly as possible I stepped forwards heavily. I couldn't believe what I'd done. I'd stepped with all my weight right on to the poor dog's paw.

It yelped loudly three times. It was like a siren going off, because everyone appeared in about five seconds flat, just in time to see the dog limping away from me.

"What did you do to Rosie?" asked Clemmie accusingly. She was leaning against Frankie, who was standing behind her, arms over Clemmie's shoulders, hands clasped over Clemmie's chest. Charlie and Mark were sitting side by side half way up the stairs. They were all nicely paired off except me. Even Dad was bending down, stroking the dog. I felt like the clumsy intruder.

She was standing in the doorway of the living-room, pushing her fingers through her hair. I noticed it then, her hair. It was neither short nor long. It came down to just below her chin in a sort of bob. If you stretched it out, it would practically touch her shoulders. Did that count? I didn't know. I'd think later.

"She'll live," *she* said casually. "Anyway, it's her own fault, romping about like that."

She turned to go but no one else moved.

"But what eggzackly did you *do* to Rosie, Sarah?" Clemmie persisted.

Something snapped inside my head.

"I didn't do anything, Clemmie!" I hissed at her. "The clumsy animal practically knocked me over."

I started to climb the stairs, struggling to get past Mark and Charlie on the way. Still no one moved. I bet they were all looking at each other. I bit my lip and felt my throat hurting. Nothing was going right. I should never have agreed to come to this place. And now they were all going to hate me, even Mark and Clemmie.

The door to the girls' room was open and I went in there, because I didn't know where else to go. There wasn't anywhere. That was the problem. I was trapped. I went over to the far corner of the room, put my hands over my face and blinked hard to stop myself from crying. I couldn't even cry in peace. There was no privacy here at all.

After a moment I looked round the room. There were two beds in it and sleeping bags on the floor for Clemmie and me. It was much bigger than my bedroom at home, all yellow and bright blue with lots of decorations. There were candles on wrought iron stands, mobiles and wind chimes. The chest of drawers was very wide, covered with pots and bottles and little photos.

Curiosity got the better of me and I took a closer look at the two photos. One was of a man I didn't recognize, but I guessed he was Charlie and Frankie's dad. He looked nice. Poor man, having a wife who left him at the drop of a hat! And now he was with someone else. It was weird to think that Charlie and Frankie visited their dad and another woman who wasn't their mother. I wondered if she'd left someone *else*. And had *that* person got a new partner? How many children all over the country went to stay with step-parents and stepbrothers and -sisters on weekends? Was it just an endless step-chain?

The other photo made me actually gasp out loud. *She* was right in the middle with her head snuggled into *my* dad's shoulder, one arm around

Frankie and the other hand resting on Charlie's shoulder. Charlie was kneeling in front, her hand reaching back to hold hands with *my* dad. All four of them wore stupid prissy smiles. Before I could stop myself I'd snatched up the photo and bashed it face down on the chest. There was a smashing sound as the glass broke. I didn't dare lift up the photo to see what the damage was. My mind was raging with anger and bitterness. I hated this step-family, even my dad, the traitor!

I waited till my heart had stopped beating then crept on to the landing. There was no sound of anyone coming upstairs so I went to have a look at the room where Mark was going to sleep. I'd got as far as the door when Dad called up the stairs.

"Mealtime, Sarah."

I stayed still and silent, until I heard his footsteps going back towards what I guessed was the kitchen. I admit I was starving, but the last thing I wanted to do was sit round a table and have a meal with that bunch downstairs. And why was Dad suddenly calling it "mealtime" anyway? He'd never said "mealtime" when he lived with us. He'd said dinner or supper. "Mealtime" was obviously one of *her* precious little words. I never did get to see the spare room because a moment later the sound of chatter and laughter came from downstairs and I knew that the kitchen door was open again.

I shot back to the girls' room, got my magazine out of my bag and lay on my side on one of the beds, pretending to be absorbed in what I was reading. I had my back to the open door, but when someone knocked on it, I just knew it was *her*. I could smell her perfume. Every muscle in my body tensed up.

5. THE FIRST MEAL
(TOO BAD IT'S NOT THE LAST)

"The lasagna's on the table, Sarah," she said. "Why don't you come and eat with us?"

I didn't move a muscle. "I'm not hungry."

She came round to the other side of the bed. I kept my eyes on the magazine.

"Don't worry, I've explained to Clemmie that of course you didn't mean to step on Rosie's foot," she said in one of those *aren't-I-a-nice-person* voices. She thought she was being so helpful. It was really getting on my nerves.

She was smiling down at me as though I was about three and a half. Was she going for the stepmother of the year award or something? I reckoned she needed to be put straight about one or two things.

"I wasn't worrying. Clemmie's my sister, remember, and I know when she's deliberately stirring things up."

"Sorry . . . I just wanted to make sure you were OK." There was a silence. I didn't look up.

"Your dad tells me you're into card tricks at the moment." Did she really think I felt like talking about my favourite hobby with *her*? I grunted and she carried on. "I love card tricks . . . and I thought we might exchange a few?"

I bet she was just making it up to show what good buddies we could be. I wished she'd just go away and leave me alone. She tried again.

"You don't want to change your mind and have something to eat?"

"No."

"The trouble is, you're sure to be hungry later, so why not just have a bite now?"

"Why can't I eat later if I'm hungry?"

"Because at the end of the meal I want to clear everything away, I'm afraid."

Her voice had hardened, which made me look up. The moment I did, she flashed me that righteous smile again as if to say, *Seems like I've won this battle*. She didn't exactly look smug, but I bet she was feeling it inside.

"Mom doesn't make me eat when I'm not hungry."

"Fine. Come down if you change your mind."

Then she went. Just like that. I could hear the galloping rhythm of her footsteps on the stairs. I flung my magazine on to the floor. I was going to have to starve now. Dad should have come up to get me. Not *her*. She can't tell me what to do and what not to do.

I went and sat on the top step to try and listen in on their conversation. All I could hear was Clemmie's voice rattling on and on, with little bursts of laughter from the others. This was Clemmie's party piece. She could turn a short anecdote into a great long rambling story, and it was guaranteed to make people laugh.

The lasagna smelt so tempting, and I was really hungry, but there was no way I could casually go downstairs and sit down at the table as though nothing had happened. Clemmie would stop mid-sentence and everyone would stare at me.

Suddenly Clemmie did stop talking and I heard Charlie's (or was it Frankie's?) shrill voice pipe up, "Is Sarah anorexic, Robert?"

My blood boiled. How *dare* she suggest such a thing to my dad! Wasn't I even allowed to miss a meal without being called anorexic by some silly girl who didn't know anything about me?

I rushed downstairs and plunged into the kitchen. Everybody looked up.

"No I am not!" I informed one of the blond girls, praying I was looking daggers at the one who had spoken.

"Charlie said it, not me," she replied calmly.

Great. I'd got the wrong one. God really had it in for me.

"Here you are, Sarah. I've put you next to your dad," *she* said, leaping to her feet and heaping lasagna on to a plate.

Dad pulled out the chair and patted it. I hesitated for a second, then went and sat down. All the chatter and laughter that I'd heard from upstairs seemed to have fizzled away, which made me look like the nasty fun-stopper. To make matters worse, Charlie, Frankie, Mark and Clemmie had to sit there and wait while I finished my lasagna before they were allowed dessert. I could feel their eyes on me, willing me to hurry up, but I couldn't go any faster. I reckoned I was already heading for an attack of indigestion. If only I could think of something witty and clever to say, to take everyone's minds (and eyes) off me! I racked my brains as I plowed through the mountain of lasagna, but everything that came into my head sounded pathetic or boring.

Eventually I pushed my plate to one side, tried not to clutch my poor stomach and mumbled, "Can't eat any more." I don't think anyone heard. They'd suddenly struck up a really interesting "flavors of ice cream" conversation.

As soon as Clemmie had noisily sucked the last spoonful of chocolate ice cream off her spoon, Frankie asked if we could leave the table and *she* nodded. I was expecting all of them to rush off upstairs, so it was quite a surprise when they started clearing the table and loading the dishwasher. Even Clemmie went proudly marching off with her ice cream bowl. I was just about to follow suit when *she* asked me a question.

"Is there anything good on television tonight, Sarah?"

Aha! Here was my chance to say something amusing.

"What do you think I am, a walking TV guide?"

The moment the words were out of my mouth, I knew I'd got it wrong. It had come out sounding really impolite and not funny at all.

Frankie and Charlie immediately began to nervously spout the entire evening's schedule, as though desperately trying to make up for my rudeness. Mark asked if he could go into the living-room.

"Yes, of course, Mark," came the reply, accompanied by a flashing smile to show how much better than mine his manners were, I presume.

And then my tactful little sister, the oh-so-popular Miss Clemmie Dale, piped up, "Has Sarah been naughty again?" She was looking round subtly, knowing very well that she was stirring up trouble, the little toad. Nobody leaped to my defence, I noticed. Dad just adopted a tired, long-suffering tone of voice.

"Go and find Mark, Clemmie." Then, more snappily, "Sarah, clear your plate away."

"I was just about to!" I protested indignantly. And as I walked over to the dishwasher I knew everyone was watching me and hating me.

"Do you want to go and watch TV with the others, Sarah?" *she* asked me in her "tolerant" voice.

"No, I'm going upstairs," I answered. There was no way of saying it without sounding sulky, so I was lost from the word go.

"Oh no you aren't, young lady," said Dad.

Something told me that he really meant business and that however humiliating it was, I ought to obey him. I kept my eyes straight ahead as I walked past Charlie and Frankie to go through to the living-room. I just hoped I hadn't gone red.

That evening was one of the worst in my life. It felt as though a knot was tightening inside me. I'd always known the weekend was going to be bad, but this was worse than my worst nightmare. If only I could rewind and start again! I was fed up with coming across as difficult. There was a bit of me that wanted Charlie and Frankie to know that I wasn't horrible and moody really, but it was too late for that. There was no turning back.

A bit later *she* asked what we all wanted to do the next day. I just stared at the TV, hoping that no one was expecting me to answer. If it had been left up to me, I would have gone home.

Whatever we did, it would be just another day of everyone getting along fine with each other except me. I tensed up as I waited for someone to answer.

"Can you drop us off in town and we'll look around the shops?" asked Charlie, while I kept my eyes glued on the TV and wondered who exactly she was talking about here. Dad's reply told me the worst.

"Sounds like a good idea," said Dad. "You and Clemmie can come with Amanda and me, Mark, while the three older girls go off together."

"OK," said Mark quickly. I wondered what was going on in his head. Maybe I'd try to get to talk to him on his own later.

Frankie didn't say anything. I bet she was thinking, *I don't want to be stuck with this moody girl*.

"What do you think, Sarah?" asked Dad in his falsely bright voice.

"Don't mind," I managed to mumble.

"Right, that's settled then," *she* said.

6. THE CONSPIRACY!

When we were having breakfast the next morning I looked at the clock and worked out how many hours I'd already spent in this nightmare and how many more were still left. Fifteen down, twenty-nine to go.

Last night I'd lain awake for ages, curled up in the cozy sleeping bag, just thinking and thinking. It had been impossible to talk to Mark in private. In fact it had been quite a challenge doing anything in private. (I'd got undressed in the bathroom in the end.)

She popped her head round the door later and whispered, "Night, everyone," but I just pretended to be asleep.

In the morning I woke up early, got dressed in the bathroom, then stood on the landing listening for noises. I couldn't be certain that no one else was up so I tiptoed downstairs and opened the kitchen door very slowly.

So far, so good. Only Rosie was in the kitchen. She was sitting in her basket, but wagged her tail and came padding over when she saw me. I sat on the floor and she lay down and rested her head on my legs.

"Sorry I stepped on your foot yesterday," I whispered as I stroked her. She made a noise as though she couldn't be bothered to bark, but didn't want to seem impolite.

It shocked me when the door opened and I looked up to see *her* standing there. She was wearing jeans and a sweatshirt and her feet were bare. I'd been hoping it would be Dad or Mark. She must have seen my disappointment because the smile kind of fell off her face. I got up and went over to the table, pretending to look at yesterday's newspaper.

"So, you're an early bird like me, are you?" she said. She was trying to sound bright, but it wasn't coming off.

"Mm," was all I could manage. I just wished she'd stop pretending to like me. It was obvious she couldn't possibly like me any more than I liked her.

I watched out of the corner of my eye as she moved around. She took a can out of a cupboard and a can-opener out of a drawer, and left them both on the side. Then she put the kettle on and walked briskly towards the washing machine.

"There you go. You can feed Rosie if you want."

I did want to feed Rosie. She felt like my only friend. I opened the can and was just about to search through all the drawers for a spoon, so that I wouldn't have to ask her where to find one, when she said, "There's a spoon in the middle drawer. Her bowl's in the utility room."

I put fresh water in Rosie's bowl and watched her digging into her food, then I went back to the newspaper.

"Looks like it's going to be a nice day," she said.

"Mm," I said without looking up. The weather had never been the most interesting subject in the world as far as I was concerned. It was a relief when Clemmie came in.

The plan was that *she* was dropping Charlie, Frankie and me off on High Street, then going back to join the others. I got into the back of the car to make quite sure I didn't have to sit in the front next to her. I was expecting either Frankie or Charlie to get into the front, but they both climbed into the back, sitting on either side of me.

"I feel like a taxi driver," she said as we drove off.

"What are the rest of you going to do while we're in town?" Charlie asked.

"I'm going to do the food shopping with Clemmie, and Robert's going to take Mark to that model railway exhibition."

I felt myself tensing up. Nobody had told me that Dad and Mark were doing something on their own. I would have much preferred to be with them. This whole thing had been arranged behind my back. It was like some kind of conspiracy.

"Can't I go with Dad and Mark?'

She sounded taken aback. "Um . . . Well, I just thought – "

"Oh no, come with us, Sarah. It'll be much more fun," interrupted Frankie.

I saw *her* smile at Frankie through the driving mirror, as if to say, *Well done, darling!* So I was right about the conspiracy. I mean, let's face it, Frankie couldn't have exactly been desperate for my company, after all that had happened, could she? It didn't take Albert Einstein to realize that she was just saying it to please her mother. It made me angry and hurt that I'd been forced into this position. It was all *her* fault for messing everything up in the first place.

I didn't reply, just shrank further down into the seat so I couldn't see her eyes through the mirror any more. I couldn't even look out of the window, stuck in the middle as I was.

The moment their mother's car pulled away, Frankie and Charlie set to work on me. It was perfectly obvious they'd been instructed to talk about the joys of step-families.

"It's lovely having a stepsister," began Frankie. She got another grunt for an answer.

"We're really lucky, aren't we?" Charlie went

on. "I mean, some children have only got one home. We've got two."

Still I didn't speak. I could feel myself tensing up again. Their words sounded so rehearsed. I mean, hadn't they ever heard of trying to be subtle? I could just imagine the conversation they must have had with their mother about how to tackle the problem of Sarah – the wrench in their plans.

Sarah's obviously finding it all a bit difficult to adapt, so I want you two to make sure she has tons of fun.

"See that dark red building in the distance, with all the glass?" said Charlie.

I followed her pointing finger.

"Uh-huh."

"That's the rec center. Mom works there. It only opened last year. It's really cool inside. You should see it!"

"We'd love to show you it one day," said Frankie.

Excuse me while I faint with joy!

Then Frankie grabbed my arm and pulled me into a massive gift shop, full of candles and mobiles and rugs and plastic blow-up chairs, and lots of other cool stuff. It was a real Aladdin's cave.

"Don't you think this place is great?" she said.

"We come in here lots," added Charlie.

"There's one like this where I live," I said casually. (It wasn't true, but I couldn't help sticking up for my home town.)

"I thought Robert said it was only a really small town where you lived," Charlie commented.

I didn't know what to say so I pretended to be really interested in some lamps. I pointed to the most expensive one.

"My friend Holly's got one like this," I said, which was completely made up.

"Mom gave me ten bucks so that we can go

to the coffee shop and have a Coke and a cake or something," said Frankie, changing the subject. "We'll take you to *Mr Beanie's*. We might see some people from our school. It'd be great if we could introduce you to our friends," she added with a big smile.

"Yeah," agreed Charlie. "We've been telling everyone at school that we've got two new stepsisters and a stepbrother."

That word *step* was really beginning to bug me. I mean, why have a word for a sister or a brother or a mother or a father who simply isn't related to you in any way whatsoever? I was Charlie's and Frankie's sister about as much as I was the President's sister. And anyway, they shouldn't be talking like that while there was still a good chance that Mom and Dad would get back together again.

They started looking at some things called "throws," and that took their minds off the *step* issue, thank goodness. I didn't even know what a throw was until I saw the picture on the front of one of the packets. It's like a sort of thin bedspread that you can throw casually over your sofa or your bed. I couldn't see the big attraction, but at least it gave me the chance to stand behind Frankie and Charlie and study them.

It was only because of their hair that they looked like twins. It was identical in length, color and thickness. The color was the best shade of golden blond anyone could want. The sun, shining through the shop window, made it glint like cut glass. I would have given anything to have hair like that. It wasn't frizzy and it wasn't too thick. When they stood close together, it looked like two gleaming curtains that hadn't been pulled together properly at the top.

"Is your dad blond too?"

I was remembering the photo next to the one

I'd smashed. I felt an instant stab of nervousness, thinking of what I'd done in a fit of temper. It was some kind of miracle, but no one seemed to have spotted it yet. I'd pay for it, of course, but I just wanted to get through the rest of the weekend without anyone noticing it, so I didn't have to apologize about it. Charlie and Frankie turned around and flashed me identical smiles, then both started talking at the same time.

"He's a bit darker than Mom."

"But apparently he used to be white blond when he was a baby."

Charlie surprised me with her next question.

"What does *your* mom look like? I bet she's pretty."

A picture of Mom standing at the front door when Dad had called to collect us came into my head. She hadn't looked pretty then. She'd looked all pointy and pinched. I tried to blink that picture away and put a different one in my head. Quite recently we'd had a drugs talk at school. It was for students and parents. At the end of it, I'd glanced over and seen Mom talking to a tall man in a leather jacket. It must have been someone's father. I'd noticed how pretty she looked at that moment.

"Yeah, she's really pretty."

"Has she got . . . you know . . . a boyfriend or anything?"

Again it was Charlie who'd spoken, and the least observant person in the whole world couldn't have missed the massive elbow in the ribs that Frankie gave her the moment the words were out of her mouth.

"No, she hasn't."

I must have spoken rather too loudly, if the stares I was getting from other shoppers were anything to go by. I just hated the way Charlie stood there and asked me so casually if Mom had a boyfriend. I wanted the golden girls to get it into their thick skulls that Mom hadn't got a boyfriend and wasn't planning on having one ever, because she and Dad would one day get back together again. What's more, if it hadn't been for *their* home-wrecking mother, *my* parents would never have split in the first place. I could feel my temper mounting. Charlie was about to get an earful and I didn't care how many people were listening. I'd never be coming back to this town again, so it didn't matter, did it?

"If you really want to know, Charlie, she hasn't got a boyfriend because she still loves my dad and she's going to get him back, so your mom had better watch out."

Charlie looked as though she was about to burst into tears, but then changed her mind and decided to fight back. "Well, that's where you're wrong, because I heard your dad talking to my mom, and he said that things would be much easier from now on because at long last your mom had got herself a boyfriend. So there!"

7. THE BEGINNING OF THE END

I felt as though Charlie had kicked me in the stomach. She sounded so sure about it. But Mom would have told me. I know she would. I looked at Frankie. She was looking down. Why wasn't she telling Charlie to stop telling lies?

"It's not true. *Is* it, Frankie?" Then I held my breath.

"We don't know anything about it really," Frankie mumbled, still looking down. "Come on, let's get out of here," she added, making her way towards the shop door. Charlie followed and I trailed after them, my heart thumping like a big bass drum.

"Don't you think I'd know if my own mother had a boyfriend?" I practically spat at them, once we were out in the street. "You must have misheard my dad . . ."

Frankie went pink and bit her lip. "Let's go to the coffee shop," she suddenly suggested. "We can talk there, Sarah."

And with that, she set off plunging through the busy street, full of rushing shoppers. Charlie followed her, tossing over her shoulder to me, "We didn't mishear, actually."

I wanted to scream out that I knew she was lying, but an old man came doddering in front of me, and I got separated from the other two. The moment there was a little gap in the crowds I caught up with them though.

"You're lying!" I spat at Charlie.

"I'm *not, am* I?" she squealed at Frankie.

"Well, we *could* have heard wrong, *couldn't* we?" Frankie hissed at Charlie, her eyes boring into her sister's. My heart seemed to be pounding in my ears now. There must be some mistake.

"I know what happened . . ." I began. But I had to stop again because we were right in the middle of the pavement, getting in everyone's way.

"Come over here," said Frankie.

We followed her down a little side street away from the cars and the noise of the Saturday crowds. It was just as though a blaring radio had been switched off. My voice sounded too loud.

"I know what happened," I tried again. "Mom must have decided to pretend to Dad that she'd got a boyfriend, so he wouldn't feel bad about taking us away from her for a whole weekend. That's what Mom's like. She thinks about other people's feelings. Especially people she loves."

Charlie put on that infuriating superior voice.

"You can get as mad as you want, Sarah. You can't change what's true. And the sooner you get used to the idea that your mom and dad don't love each other any more, the better," she said.

I was speechless. How dare she! And what made me maddest of all was the way she was acting like she was the grown-up and I was a little girl. I was about to tell her where to get off, when Frankie started talking in the same pious tone.

"I found it quite hard at first . . ." she said, tipping her silly head on one side. "But you get used to it, and then you'll find it's fine. Honestly."

I felt like hitting her. Instead I told her precisely what I thought of her words of wisdom.

"I'm not the same as you two, thank goodness. And you don't know anything about my mom or my dad. Dad might be living with your mom, but he's *my* dad, not yours, so you'd better get that inside your thick skulls."

Frankie was looking around frantically. Maybe she was trying to spot a passing fairy with a magic wand, who could put everything right instantly.

"What time is it?" Charlie suddenly asked Frankie.

"Ten past ten. Nearly two hours to go," Frankie replied.

I turned on her.

"I thought you loved it in town. I thought you were dying to show me everything, but you're not interested in me at all, are you? You're just putting up with me because your mom told you to. And I presume she was the one who told you both to go on about how wonderful it is to have two homes and all that. Well, you can tell her from me that her little plan failed miserably. She's a home-wrecker. She's ruined my family and nothing you can say will make it better." I could feel the tears gathering behind my eyes, waiting until I could get away, so they could fall. "I'm off. Thanks for a truly great time."

"Where are you going?" Frankie called after me.

She sounded pretty worried then. Good. Served her right. I didn't even bother to turn around, just rushed back onto High Street and hurried through the crowds until I was sure I couldn't be seen any more. Then I plunged into a bookshop and pretended to be looking at books. My throat hurt with the effort of crying in silence and I had to be careful not to let any tears fall on the pages.

Every so often I took a quick look out of the window to check that I wasn't being spied on by the golden girls. One time when I looked up I saw that a green bus had stopped right outside. A plan was forming in my head. Yes! Why shouldn't I? I put down the book I was holding and rushed out of the shop.

"Excuse me," I said to the bus driver, "but can you tell me what number bus I need to get to Stoughton?"

"Forty-two," he answered. "And this is it! Must be your lucky day!"

It hadn't been very lucky so far, I thought. But maybe my luck was about to change. I gave him the bus fare then went to the very back of the bus and shrank down in the corner, away from prying, spying eyes.

8. KEEPING SECRETS

It was morning recess, and Lauren, Holly, Katie, Kelly and I were in the library. We were supposed to be outside really because it was nice out, but Katie had insisted we come to the library.

"See," she said, as we sat down at a table which was tucked round a corner, neatly out of sight of the door, "this is much better than standing out there with everybody listening."

She was grinning around at us as though she'd managed to reserve the best table in a posh restaurant.

"Tell us all about it, Sarah. We've been dying to know," whispered Holly, leaning forwards.

"Yeah, quick, before the bell goes," hissed Kelly, throwing surreptitious glances over her shoulder, like a spy checking out for enemy presence.

"Well, basically, I hate *her* more than ever now," I began dramatically.

Katie's eyes widened. "Do you mean . . . ?" She pulled out the crumpled piece of paper, on which was written the name *Amanda*, and thrust it under my nose.

I nodded and pulled a face. "I didn't even stay the full weekend. I caught a bus home on Saturday morning, because I'd had enough."

Gasps went up when I said that and then they started hurling question after question at me. Didn't anyone try to stop you? Did you tell anyone, or did you just go? Then, what did Charlie and Frankie and their mother look like? How had Mark and Clemmie reacted? What was the house like? What did you all do? Everything!

I found myself enjoying answering all their questions because they were so interested and caring. I didn't think I'd ever been the centre of attention like this before. It felt good when they frowned and nodded, saying things like, "Don't blame you, Sare," and "Good for you! That told *her*!"

In the end, we were all laughing, even though I had just been through the weekend from hell. But then Kelly asked me the question I'd been dreading.

"What did your mom say when you got home?"

I tried to look as casual as possible and told my first lie.

"She left a message on the home-wrecker's answering machine, to tell Dad that I was safely home, then she and I had a really nice time together for the rest of the weekend."

"So what's going to happen the weekend after

next when you have to go back again?" Katie asked.

"I wouldn't go back there if you paid me," I told her through clenched teeth.

"Not even for five hundred dollars?" asked Holly.

"Well, maybe for five hundred dollars," I said, "but not a penny less!"

Everyone laughed. After that we talked about my birthday which was in a few days' time. I wasn't looking forward to it as much as I usually did, although it was exciting to think that I was about to be a teenager.

Lauren and I caught the bus after school. We both got off at my stop because we'd decided to do our homework together. It had been Lauren's idea. The trouble was, I know Lauren, and I didn't reckon homework was the only thing on her agenda.

"What *really* happened when you got home

on Saturday, Sare?" she asked me quietly when we were up in my room with glasses of milk and a plate of cookies.

I sighed a big sigh. I hadn't intended to tell anyone the awful truth, but somehow, Lauren's wide blue eyes, fixing me with such a sympathetic gaze, made me spill it all out.

"Oh Lauren, it was awful! I let myself in through the back door. Mom wasn't in the kitchen so I went through to the living-room. And there she was. Only she wasn't alone. She was sitting on the sofa with a man, and he had his arm round her. I just stared at them with my mouth open."

"Who was he?" asked Lauren quietly.

"His name's Steve and he's the father of some- one in grade eleven. I saw him and Mom talking to each other at that drugs talk we had. I'd no idea they were . . . you know . . ."

"Going out with each other," Lauren finished

off the sentence. I nodded, and felt the tears welling up in my eyes for about the tenth time in three days. "I don't know what's the matter with me. I just feel like crying all the time," I told Lauren.

"What did your mom say to you when you walked in on them like that?"

"She jumped up and went all red, and started chattering at me, like a battery-operated toy."

Lauren giggled. "But what did she say?"

I put on a high-pitched voice and gave her an exaggerated imitation of the way Mom had reacted.

"Omigod! Sarah! What are you doing here? What's happened? Where are the others? I thought you weren't coming home till tomorrow. Omigod! Omigod! This is Steve. He's a friend of mine. I was going to tell you about him. Omigod!"

By this time Lauren was really shaking with

laughter. "I can just imagine the scene. I bet you gave her the shock of her life."

"Yeah, but it wasn't half as big as the shock she gave me."

"So what did you say when you saw them together?"

"I said something like, 'Oh great! Both my parents are acting like pathetic teenagers, and one of them hasn't even got the guts to tell me. But don't worry, I'm only your daughter. I'm sure I'll just love the wonderful new life that you and Dad are sorting out behind my back!' Then I stormed out, ran up to my room and threw myself on to my bed. I knew I was acting like a spoiled little kid having a tantrum, Lauren, but I felt so hurt. I hated that they were keeping secrets from me. Big, important secrets that concerned me."

"So you don't even know what he's like – this Steve?" said Lauren gently.

"No. And I don't want to. I wish everything could just go back to how it was before."

Lauren put her arm round me.

"At least you didn't get told off. My mom would have killed me if I'd done what you did."

"Don't you believe it. As soon as Mom had got over the shock of me walking in on her and Steve, she started going mad. I mean, *big* time. She gave me a massive lecture on the dangers of traveling on my own and all the things that might have happened to me. Then she went on about how worried Dad and everyone must have been. I let her rant and rave for a while then I told her my side of the story. I laid it on really thick about how awful it was being forced into spending a whole weekend with people you don't even like."

"And what about your dad?"

"When he phoned on Saturday, I told Mom I didn't want to speak to him because I'd only get another big lecture. Mom said that Dad *had* been very mad, but that he'd calmed down now and just wanted to talk to me. But I didn't believe her."

"So didn't you speak to him?"

"No."

Lauren said that she was sure everything would turn out OK in the end. I told her that things certainly couldn't be any worse. And that's when the phone rang and Mom came up to tell me that Dad had called to see if I'd like to go swimming and then out for a meal with him for my birthday on Thursday.

"Apparently he's got you a present that he knows you'll absolutely love!" she said, looking at me with a rather nervous smile as though she thought I might suddenly go off at the deep end. "He's not mad anymore, honestly," she added, when I didn't say anything straight away.

"Is *she* coming out with us?" I asked.

"Dad didn't mention her . . . so I don't know," Mom replied.

I felt pleased that Dad wanted to take me out. I guessed he'd probably have a bit of a go at me, but he couldn't go totally beserk on my birthday, could he? Maybe he'd finally got the message that I wasn't up for playing "Big Happy Family" at someone else's house. Perhaps this would be a good chance to try and explain my point of view to him. I didn't really care too much about the birthday present.

"Well, I'll go as long as it's just me and Dad," I said.

"I told Dad you'd phone him back to let him know," she said, with a bit of a question mark in her voice. "You could ask him about Amanda then," she added.

"I've told you, I'm not phoning *her* house. Can't you call him?"

"Yes, all right," said Mom, as she crept out

and shut the door gently behind her.

"Don't be too hard on your mom," said Lauren, pretending to study the lyric sheet from one of my CDs.

I didn't reply. It was nice to have Lauren's friendship, but I didn't want her acting like my counselor.

9. BIRTHDAY TREAT!

Because neither Mom nor I mentioned the name Steve after that awful Saturday, I started to think that maybe I'd just dreamt the whole thing, or that Steve was simply a figment of my imagination. Mark and Clemmie quite obviously didn't have a clue that Mom had a new "friend". So Monday turned to Tuesday and Tuesday turned to Wednesday, and I grabbed the phone every time it rang, and it was never Steve. Surely if he'd been mom's boyfriend he would have called by now? Perhaps he wasn't her boyfriend.

Maybe he was just an ordinary friend. I knew I could easily ask Mom, but I didn't want to hear the worst and I thought if the name Steve never passed my lips, he might slip quietly out of our lives.

Mark and I had had one conversation about the weekend. He'd asked me why I'd "run away" as he put it, and I'd told him I hated being forced into being with people I didn't want to be with and doing things I didn't want to do.

"I just don't think it's fair that I've got no choice," I said. "And anyway, I can't get used to the idea of Dad being with someone else. I feel sorry for Mom."

"Yeah, me too," said Mark, glumly. "I wish *she'd* get a new friend, and then everything would seem fairer."

(I didn't mention Steve. Mark would find out soon enough.)

"But don't you think it would be better if Mom

and Dad were back together and we were all a family like we used to be?" I asked him, desperately hoping he'd agree.

"I dunno. Billy Sharp's mom and dad have split up and Billy says it's much better now because there aren't so many arguments going on all the time. Billy says he didn't like his new stepdad or his new stepmom at first, but now he thinks they're OK."

I suddenly needed to know what Mark thought about *her*.

"Do you like . . . you know . . . ?"

"Amanda?"

I nodded.

"Not really."

Well, that was something.

"Neither do I," I told him, hoping that we might be able to exchange a few "revolting stepmother" stories. But Mark quickly put me straight on that.

"I expect we'll like her soon though. Once we're sure that Mom doesn't mind . . . And Frankie and Charlie are OK, aren't they? I mean, they're not all girlie or anything."

My spirits took a dive. It felt like my one and only ally had been slowly disappearing and now he had gone for sure. Apart from Mark there was only Clemmie, and you couldn't have a proper conversation with Clemmie. She was getting more and more into poetry. Who knows what they'd been doing at school. It was ridiculous!

You'd say, "Can you pass the salt, Clemmie?" and she'd say, "Pass the salt. That's your fault."

"What's on TV?"

"Something icky."

I once said "Don't be silly," and the moment the words were out of my mouth I regretted it. I was expecting Clemmie to laugh like a hyena when she did a rhyme for that one, but being

Clemmie, she didn't think of the obvious one. Instead she came out with, "Your name's Billy," and I wished for a moment that I was still six years old and that nothing was more complicated than having to find a rhyme for "silly".

On Thursday morning I was woken by my totally over-the-top little sister, singing "Happy birthday to you, Happy birthday to you, Happy birthday dear Sarah, bear-ah," (giggle, giggle, chuckle, laugh hysterically), "Happy birthday to you!"

When I opened my eyes, there were Clemmie, Mark and Mom all standing in a row, clutching presents. I felt a fleeting sadness, because Dad had always been in the line-up before. I could have got myself all wound up about the home-wrecker if Clemmie hadn't brought me back to the here and now.

"I'm first, 'cuz I'm the youngest," she said, clambering on to my bed and handing me a large package tied up with red ribbon. There was also a whole cluster of red ribbons decorating the top of the parcel. I figured Clemmie had just discovered how to make ribbon curl with scissors, and she'd got a bit carried away.

"It was me what did all them curls," she told me, grinning proudly.

"It was *I who* did all *those* curls," Mom corrected.

Clemmie looked up in surprise. "No you didn't, Mom. I did."

I unwrapped layer after layer of newspaper and finally found the present inside. It was a green kangaroo. From behind Clemmie, Mom mouthed, "She insisted!" and rolled her eyes at the ceiling. Clemmie was grinning at me, obviously waiting for me to fall out of bed with happiness.

"It's lovely, Clemmie! Thank you very much. Just what I wanted,' I assured her chirpily, as I gave her a big hug. Then Clemmie turned to Mom and said "See!" in a very accusing voice. "Now it's Mark's turn."

Not that I didn't love Clemmie's sweet present, but Mark's was just right. It was a beautiful scented candle and a little colored pot for putting things in.

"They're beautiful, Mark. Thank you very much."

"And now for my present," said Mom, handing me an envelope. "Read what it says."

Inside the envelope was a card which said, *Happy Birthday, darling. Sorry your present won't be here till Saturday, but here's something to keep you going.* A twenty dollar bill came fluttering out on to my bed.

"Thanks, Mom . . . but why Saturday?"

"Ha ha! You'll see." She gave me a big hug. "I can't believe you're thirteen. It doesn't seem a minute since you were rushing around in diapers."

So now I could look forward to two presents – one from Dad this evening and one from Mom on Saturday. I was feeling quite relaxed about the evening because Dad had told Mom on the phone that *she* wasn't going to be able to come on the outing. When he'd said that I'd felt like giving three cheers, but I decided it wouldn't go down very well, so I'd kept quiet and just grinned to myself.

At school, I got a CD of my favourite single from Kelly, a picture frame and some lipstick from Katie, a cool set of writing paper and envelopes from Holly and a book of card tricks from Lauren. They were all great presents, but my favorite was the book of card tricks because I'd always loved every sort of magic, but card tricks were definitely my "thing" at the moment.

Back at home, after school, I found three presents on the kitchen table – one from Auntie

Steph, one from Mrs Bingham our next-door-neighbor, and one from Granny and Grandad.

Dad was picking me up at half-past five. By five o'clock I was all ready and waiting, swimming things packed. Butterflies were dancing about in the pit of my stomach. I knew they'd be whirling and swirling by the time the car pulled up, because I'd decided to try and have a real heart-to-heart with Dad. I was also quite excited about what the mysterious present might be.

I wondered if Dad had remembered a conversation that had taken place before he and Mom had split up. I'd been telling them how lots of my friends at school had got their own cell phones, which meant that their parents could contact them whenever they wanted. Mom had said I was too young, and that I'd have to just wait for one (!) and Dad had said, "You're not even a teenager, Sarah. There's plenty of time for all that kind of thing."

So right now, I was secretly hoping that maybe – just maybe – Dad had decided to get me one, as I was now a full-fledged teenager.

"Why is Dad going out with Sarah scarer and not with me and Mark shark? It's not fair, Mom tom."

"It's only just this one time, Clemmie. It's a special occasion, Sarah's birthday, and Dad thought it would be a nice treat. And *please* stop making everything rhyme. It's driving me up the wall."

I was really hoping that Clemmie would drop the subject of going out with Dad, because if she complained for long enough, Mom might give in and say, "Oh, all right, I'll phone Dad and you can all go." I wasn't being selfish or anything, but just for once I wanted Dad to myself.

I watched for Dad's car from my bedroom window. When five-thirty came and went, I began to worry. I shot downstairs to Mom.

"He did say half-past five, didn't he?" I double-checked.

"Yes, don't worry. He'll be here any minute." I raced up the stairs again and as I got to the top I heard the bell ring, so I rushed back down again. By then, Dad was in the kitchen. I was suddenly embarrassed because of course we hadn't seen each other since the disastrous weekend. Dad was all smiles though, so I tried to forget about the past, and just look forward to this evening. He gave me a big hug.

"How's my thirteen-year-old doing?" he asked, lifting me off my feet and spinning me round. "Any changes?" He pretended to study my face really closely. "Yes, I think I detect a bit of ageing!"

"Can I come too, Dad?" asked Clemmie.

I held my breath.

"Not today, Clemms. This is Sarah's birthday treat." I let out my breath. "All ready, Sarah?"

I nodded and off we went, everyone calling out 'bye to each other.

"Where are we going, Dad?" I asked as I opened the passenger door.

"A beautiful restaurant that I'm sure will be to Madam's taste," Dad replied. He'd put on a really posh voice as though he were the chauffeur. It was just the kind of jokey thing he always used to do when he lived at home with us. I felt another little stab of pain, that now it was Frankie and Charlie who had Dad's cool sense of humor with them all the time, not me. And all because their mom had taken my dad away from our family! I tried to shake the horrible thoughts away. I didn't want anything to spoil this precious evening.

I noticed we were heading towards the city where *she* lived but I tried not to feel too fed up; after all, this road led to all sorts of other places too. Dad and I chatted about this and that —

school mainly – but he never said a word about last weekend, and neither did he mention any of the three names I didn't want to hear. He must have decided I'd had enough scolding from Mom.

"Are we going to Boston, Dad?" I asked a few minutes later.

"We certainly are. So get ready to take 'em by storm!"

I couldn't help laughing because of the funny gruff voice Dad put on, and the way he hunched his shoulders up as though he was imitating one of the bad guys in a gangster movie. But a little warning bell was ringing in the back of my mind, stopping me from relaxing, even as I laughed.

We were approaching a large dark red building, with loads of bright glistening windows. The warning bells were getting louder inside my head. Why did I recognize this place? We pulled up in the parking lot really close to the main doors, and my heart sunk as my hackles rose. I remembered now where I'd seen this building before. It was the rec center, and from out of its wide swing doors, wreathed in smiles, came the home-wrecker.

10. THE CANDLES

"You told me *she* wasn't coming," I said to Dad.

"No, she's not. She's just saying Happy Birthday," Dad replied, still in his bright voice. "Come on, out you go. Just wait till you see the pool!"

As we were getting out she kissed Dad then came grinning around to my side of the car and patted my arm awkwardly.

"Happy birthday, Sarah."

She kept her nauseating smile in place, like a well-trained chimpanzee, but I knew it wasn't genuine because she must have hated my guts after I'd abandoned her precious daughters on the weekend. A part of me wished that she and Dad would just get angry and then I could shout back at them. It was embarrassing the way they were both acting as though nothing had happened and we were all cozy together.

"Right, I've had enough of this place for one day," she said jokingly. "I'm off home."

"Unless you want to stay and have a dip in the pool with Sarah and me?" said Dad.

I could have killed him. He knew very well I didn't want her with us. In fact I didn't want to share anything with *her*, but especially not my birthday treat. I looked down at the ground. A bubble of anger was growing inside me, but fortunately she stepped in before it got too big.

"No, no . . . I said I wasn't coming swimming and I'm sticking to that. You two go and have some fun together and I'll see you later."

I couldn't believe my ears. Part of me felt like putting a big scowl on my face and saying, *What do you mean, "later"?* Part of me felt like bursting into tears and asking to go home. But that would make me look pathetic. Part of me – the biggest part – felt like giving Dad my hardest look and saying, *You haven't got a clue, have you?*

As these thoughts flashed through my mind, a little voice was trying to make itself heard above all my anger. *Keep calm*, it said. *You'll only spoil everything if you fly off the handle.* So I forced my mouth into a smile, adopted a kind of blank stare, and probably ended up looking like a retarded toad.

"Come on then, Sarah," said Dad, plunging in through the swing doors. "Bye, Mand," he called over his shoulder. "See you at eight-fifteen."

Dad paid for the swimming tickets then set off upstairs.

"The changing rooms are over there, Dad," I

said, pointing to the sign at the far end of Reception.

"Yes, I know, but I want to show you something first," he said mysteriously.

Feeling like Mr. Miserable being scooped up by Mr. Happy and whirled into Happyland, I followed him up the stairs. At the top was a thickly carpeted corridor, glass-paneled on both sides. On one side we looked down on five or six freshly painted, gleaming squash courts. All of them were occupied. Sweating people were slamming tiny balls at the walls, leaping and diving as though their lives depended on it.

"Mad fools!" joked Dad. "You wouldn't catch me killing myself like that!" He put his arm round my shoulder and turned me round to face the other side. "There's a great new theater down there. Shame we can't see it. Amanda says it's really spectacular, and apparently they attract some very big names, for a rec center."

I was just wondering what on earth was the point of all this, when Dad went leaping off again, up another flight of stairs. I had a job keeping up with him. At the top we entered another glass-paneled corridor.

"There," he said, and I followed his gaze.

This time I was genuinely speechless. We were looking down from a great height onto the most amazing-looking swimming pool I thought I'd ever seen. It was really three swimming pools in one, with an incredible spiral water slide that seemed to uncoil right from the ceiling to the blue-green water far below, like a giant snake.

There were lots of people swimming, jumping about and playing, their voices rising in squeaks and squeals above the swish of the wave machine. Then there was a diving area with three boards of different heights, and finally a huge area where the water lapped over the palm green bottom of the pool, then got gradually deeper, just like the sea. There was a little island of exotic plants and the people swimming round it were carried on a faster current. The whole thing was out of this world, and for a moment I forgot where I was.

"It looks amazing. Especially the slide," I said.

"Yes, that's Charlie's and my favorite thing," said Dad enthusiastically. "Going down two at a time's a bit scary though, I can tell you!"

He'd done it again. It was just as though I'd started the evening with a dozen candles burning warm and bright inside me, then we'd met *her* and six of them had promptly gone out. Now he'd just blown out another one, with his throw-away comment about what he did with her daughters. He'd never been down a slide with *me* before, and I was his real daughter!

"Right, let's take the plunge," said Dad brightly.

But I wasn't in the mood any more. I was too fed up to jump and splash and slide and swim.

"I don't really feel like it actually," I said in a flat voice.

Dad's face fell but he was obviously determined that nothing would make any dents in our happy-go-lucky evening. Huh!

"Well, is there anything else you feel like doing? What about the jacuzzi?"

I wanted to know whether he'd ever been to the jacuzzi with Charlie, but I knew I was just being childish and pathetic.

"I'm quite hungry," I said hesitantly.

"OK, let's go straight to the restaurant."

As we drove along I began to feel a bit happier. There was a good chance that *she* might not be able to manage this earlier time. I didn't know whether Charlie and Frankie had to have a baby-sitter or whether they were old enough to be left on their own.

"Have Charlie and Frankie got a sitter?" I asked.

"Oh, good point. Thanks for reminding me, Sarah. I must give Amanda a ring. Good thing you mentioned that." He punched in the number and then turned to me, while he waited. "No, Charlie and Frankie are with their dad this evening."

Another candle went out inside me.

"Mand? Hi, it's me," he said with a stupid smile on his face as though she could see him. "We decided not to swim after all, so we're making our way to the restaurant. Meet you there? . . . Uh-huh . . . Yep . . . OK, see you soon."

As we went into the restaurant I realized that Dad must have chosen this one specially for me, because it was so similar to a place that I really love, in Stoughton, called Racklins. It cheered me up instantly.

"Oh, it's just like Racklins, isn't it?" I said looking round happily. "Good choice, Dad. I love all the beams and the dried flowers."

He looked pleased.

"Aman . . . I'm glad you like it. Great!"

He'd tried to cover up his mistake but it hadn't worked. He was going to say that *she'd* chosen the restaurant, not him. Another candle went out. I gritted my teeth and thought hard about my new resolution and the cell phone, as we studied the menu and discussed the various starters and main courses.

We were still engrossed in the menus when she came in, all wreathed in smiles and stinking of perfume. She'd changed into black velvet pants and a clingy white top. I saw Dad look at her as though she was Miss World. She was giggling by the time she reached the table.

"Look, we're all dressed in black and white," she said as she sat down. (Unfortunately, it was true.) "Do you think people will think we've come thematically dressed on purpose?" she giggled.

Raucous laughter from Dad. I raised my menu

higher to cover my face, but Dad was determined to try and get me to laugh.

"That reminds me — tell Sarah that joke you told me yesterday," he said to her.

"OK. What goes black, white, black, white, black, white . . . ?"

We never did hear the answer because the waitress turned up and asked us if we were ready to order.

When we'd all said what we wanted (I chose smoked salmon and lemon chicken), Dad took an envelope out of his inside jacket pocket and handed it to me with a big grin on his face.

"Many happy returns, Sarah."

"Happy birthday again!" she added.

The card had a picture of a hedgehog on it. I opened it and saw that all four of them had signed their names. Another little candle went out inside me.

"And your present is something that we both

know you're going to love, but I'm afraid you can't have it until a week from Saturday, when you're over with us, next time."

I tried to ignore the "week-from-Saturday" bit and concentrate on the present.

"Can't you just tell me what it is?" I asked, clasping my hands as though in prayer and giving him my best pleading look.

" 'Fraid not," said Dad, laughing.

"We could let her guess though, couldn't we?" *she* said, and for a second I forgot I didn't like her.

"Yes, twenty questions. You're only allowed to answer yes or no," I jabbered excitedly.

"OK, shoot!" said Dad.

"Is it something I've been interested in for about a year?"

"Yes," they both answered together.

"Is it very small?"

"No," said Dad.

"Well . . . it *is* very small in a way, Robert."

"Mm. It depends which way you look at it."

I was racking my brains to try and work out how a cell phone could be seen as very small and yet not very small. A candle was flickering, waiting to die. A cell phone was definitely small. There were no two ways about it. The disappointment must have shown on my face.

"Oh dear, I'm afraid it's not what you thought it was," said Dad, looking sympathetic. "But I know you'll like what we've got you even more than a cell phone."

There, he'd said it. My dream wasn't about to come true, after all. The flickering candle went out.

"Oh, what a shame, Sarah. Your father and I discussed a mobile phone, but we decided that it would be better to wait until you're fourteen, because that's when Frankie's going to be allowed to have one. We thought it would be fairer to keep things even for all three of you, you see . . ."

I saw red when she said that. Blood red.

"What's Frankie got to do with me?" I blurted out. "She's not my sister, and *you're* not my mother." My voice got louder. "I just wish you'd stop interfering with things that have got nothing to do with you." My temper was rising and there was absolutely nothing I could do to stop it. I turned on Dad, practically shouting.

"*She* chose the restaurant, didn't she? You couldn't even do that for me, could you? I bet you would have done it for Charlie or Frankie, wouldn't you? You make everything good fun for them, don't you, going down slides and having a great time?"

I knew I was sounding hysterical but nothing could stop me now. Dad was mouthing "*Ssh!*" and holding his hand out nervously in a sort of "*Keep calm, Sarah*" gesture. *She* was looking down, lips pursed.

"Well, you can keep your birthday present," I went on in a louder voice. "I don't want it. And you can keep this too." I chucked the card at him. "Thanks very much for a lovely evening!"

That made her look up. They were both staring at me like statues with moving eyes. The whole restaurant had gone quiet as though I'd pressed a "pause" button and stopped the world. For a second I didn't know what to do, but then I just walked out, knowing they had to follow me. I hoped they were really embarrassed. It served them right.

The last candle went out as I pushed open the door. It was dark outside. And dark inside.

11. NO ESCAPE ROUTE

Lauren, Holly, Katie and Kelly looked horrified. We were all sitting in the classroom before roll-call on Friday morning, and I'd just been telling them about my unbelievable birthday dinner.

"Did your dad and . . . you know who . . . come straight out after you, or what?" asked Holly.

"Dad followed me straight out and tried to calm me down, and she came out a minute later."

"Did you talk in the car?" asked Katie.

"Not until Dad pulled up outside Mom's."

"What did he say then?"

"He asked if I wanted him to come in and have a word with Mom, and I said I could manage my own words, thank you very much. Then he said he'd call later, and I went without saying 'bye to either of them."

There was a silence when I stopped talking, then Kelly spoke.

"Well, that certainly told *her*, didn't it?"

She looked round at the others and they all nodded vigorously, except Lauren, who was looking down.

"Are you supposed to be going to your dad's this weekend?" asked Holly.

"No," I replied. "Mark's going though, but only tomorrow because he's got a party on Sunday. He can't make the following weekend because of his football play-offs."

"Does Mark like going over to your dad's?"

"He said he didn't mind going tomorrow because it's only for one day. But Mark doesn't hate *her* as much as I do. That's because he's too young to realize that she's trying to take Mom's place. Once he realizes that, he'll soon change his mind."

"So, you're going the following weekend, are you?" asked Katie.

"Not if *she's* going to be there. No."

"But what about your present?'

"I don't know if I'm getting that now. When Dad phoned up late last night, he told Mom what the present is. Apparently it's tickets to something or other, that we're supposed to be seeing next weekend, but he didn't think I deserved any more treats after the way I'd just behaved. He said he'd phone in a couple of days to see what I had to say for myself. If he thinks I'm going to apologize, he can forget it."

"So what are you going to say?" asked Lauren.

I shrugged. "Dunno."

"Don't you think it would be better just to apologize?"

I couldn't tell if Lauren meant that I should apologize because it was my fault, or because it would make life easier. I didn't find out until recess because the teacher appeared at that point and we all got into our places.

At break time Lauren and I went to the snack machine together and on the way she told me she felt a bit sorry for *her*. (Lauren actually called her by her name.)

"How *can* you?" I asked her, horrified that my best friend seemed to be defending the person I hated most in the whole world.

"Well, if they'd given you the cell phone for your birthday it might have seemed as though they were trying to buy your love, instead of earning it. I mean, it would have been sucking up to you, wouldn't it, giving you exactly what you wanted?"

"Listen Lauren, I hate the woman. How can

you talk to me about love?"

"Well your dad loves you and she loves him, so that's quite a bit of love, isn't it?"

Sometimes Lauren completely misses the point. And right now was one of those times.

"Since when did you become such an authority on separation?" I asked her. As soon as the words were out of my mouth I felt bad because she looked so shocked and sad all of a sudden. "Sorry, Lauren, it's just that I'm really upset about it all, and I don't think anyone can properly understand how I feel unless they're going through exactly the same thing."

On Saturday morning I woke up feeling excited, because this was the day I was getting my birthday present from Mom. I still didn't know why I'd had to wait till today. It was all very mysterious.

At nine o'clock Dad arrived to collect Mark.

He and Clemmie were upstairs and I was practicing card tricks when Dad came into the kitchen. Mom offered him a coffee and he accepted. I was surprised, because he and Mom seemed to be acting so normal with each other. Ever since the break-up the looks they'd exchanged had been cold, and whenever they spoke to each other, it was in a hard tone. I couldn't help wondering whether this sudden change might mean they were thinking of getting back together again. I watched and listened carefully, pretending I wasn't taking any notice.

"Great coffee, Debra," said Dad, and he actually winked at Mom.

"Well, thank you, Robert," Mom replied, smiling right into his face.

They were sharing some sort of a private joke and I'd no idea what it was about. But it didn't matter. I felt like jumping on to the table and dancing a jig, because this was exactly the way they always used to be before *she* came along and ruined it all. In fact I felt so happy that I impulsively decided to apologize.

"Sorry about Thursday, Dad."

Mom turned her back and started cleaning the sink. Dad lowered his head and looked at me as though he was wearing glasses and looking over the tops of them. He was waiting for me to go on but I didn't know what else to say.

"I . . . I was just upset, that's all," I stammered.

"It would be a great deal better for everyone if you wouldn't keep flying off the handle, Sarah. I was so ashamed of you."

I bit my lip and looked down. I'd been expecting instant forgiveness, so this mini lecture came as quite a shock.

"But why can't we do something on our own for once?" I blurted out.

"That's what we've been doing for the past ten months, Sarah." He paused, presumably to let it sink in. "You might be interested to know that Amanda didn't think she ought to come with us on Thursday evening. It was my idea that she did. I really wanted her to come swimming too, but she said that she thought you'd prefer it without her. It took a lot of persuasion to get her to come to the meal. I knew you didn't want her to be there, but I somehow hoped that once we were in the restaurant, everything would be fine. Amanda insisted that it would be a mistake and it turned out that she was absolutely right."

Dad's words had made me feel strange. I wasn't sure what the feeling was exactly. All I knew was that I didn't have the energy to argue or to say anything, so I stayed still and stared at the floor.

After a few seconds he started admiring my card trick book. He must have thought that was enough of picking-on-Sarah for one session. Then Clemmie and Mark came in and everyone started talking at once, Clemmie dancing round

Dad and singing *Here we go round the daddy pie*.

"Have a good day, everyone," Dad said a few minutes later as he went out with Mark. "I'll phone during the week," he added, smiling at me. I gave a sort of half-smile back but didn't say anything. I still had that funny feeling. I suppose it was guilt, now that I'd heard Dad's side of the story.

At five-past ten there was a knock at the door. Mom answered it, and I had the sudden fantastic thought that maybe Dad had come back, and he'd only been pretending to collect Mark, but really Mom and Dad were going to surprise me by taking us all out for the day. My wonderful castle in the air collapsed in a heap on the floor when I saw who was coming into the kitchen.

It was Steve, looking totally stupid in my opinion, in a leather jacket and jeans.

"Hi," he said.

I glared at Mom, gathered up all my cards as quickly as I could and made for the kitchen door. Unfortunately my adorable little sister chose that moment to crash her way in, so we collided in the doorway and my cards went flying everywhere.

"Well done, Clemmie," I said through gritted teeth. Then, unbelievably, without a word of apology to me, she hurled herself at Steve, who scooped her up and whizzed her round above his head. He's very tall and muscular, so he looked as though he was playing with his toy helicopter. Clemmie was making a noise like a howling wolf with hiccups. She really was far too excited for her own good. Mom was grinning at the pair of them like a Cheshire cat.

"Don't worry, I'll pick them all up," I informed the assembled gathering in my most sarcastic tones. And guess what? In no time at all, all three of them were on their hands and knees, collecting up cards as though their lives depended on it. I said "thank you" in a voice so low that I doubted anyone heard, then went up to my room, lay on my bed and thought what to do.

First it was Dad and *her*. Now it was Mom and *him*. I felt as though I'd climbed to the top of some high rocks in the middle of a beach, and then the tide had come in and I'd realized there was no way off the rocks on one side, but it didn't matter because there was nothing preventing me from climbing down the other side. But then the worst possible thing had happened. The sea had crept up without my noticing and surrounded the whole island, and the tide was still rising higher. I was trapped. Stuck with no escape route.

12. THE JACKSON FAMILY

"Hi, Tricia. Could I speak to Lauren, please?"

"I'm sorry, Sarah, she's gone to her grand-parents' for the day. Didn't she tell you? Shall I get her to call you when she gets back this evening?"

"Um . . . no, it doesn't matter. Thanks anyway."

I punched in Holly's number next.

"Hello, can I speak to Holly, please?"

"Holly's at her piano lesson, and then she's going into town. She'll be back this afternoon."

"Oh, OK. I'll try later."

I dialed Katie's number and listened to twenty-three rings before replacing the receiver, and finally I tried Kelly's number and crossed my fingers until Kelly's dad called out loudly, "Kelly! Phone."

"Hi, Kelly. It's me . . . Sarah."

"Hi, Sarah." She didn't sound all that pleased to hear from me.

"Are you doing anything today?"

"Yeah, I'm being severely nagged by my dad, but that's nothing new."

"At least he's your dad and not your mom's new boyfriend," I said, feeling dangerously close to tears.

"Well, actually I'm getting grief from Mom too."

It was funny, but as Kelly was talking, I was thinking how lucky she was. How nice it would be to get grief and nagging from both parents at the same time!

"Mom's new boyfriend has just turned up and I don't feel like staying here while he's around," I went on.

"You can come to my place if you want."

"Thanks, Kelly. I was hoping you'd say that," I admitted, feeling about a million times better. "I'll be there in twenty minutes."

"OK. Seeya."

Normally I would ask Mom if it was all right for me to go to a friend's house, but this time, I decided to tell her I was going. After all, she did things without asking my permission. I listened outside the kitchen door before I went in. I could hear all three voices but I couldn't make out what was being said.

When I got in, they were all crouched on the floor near the sink.

"Look, Sarah," said Clemmie. "Steve's found two grasshoppers. It's sprizin' to find *one*, you know, but two is really 'sepchunelle!'"

It was obvious that Clemmie was quoting the wonderful Steve. She didn't have a clue what exceptional meant. She couldn't even pronounce it properly. Clemmie seemed to be really hitting it off with Steve, in true Clemmie fashion.

"I'm going to Kelly's, Mom."

"Oh . . . Right. When are you coming back?"

"Dunno."

"Where does she live? Do you need a lift?" asked Steve.

"I'm walking," I told him.

Mom seemed to gather herself. "Sorry, Sarah, but that's not good enough. Steve and I are taking you and Clemmie out for lunch. I'd rather you didn't go making arrangements without asking me first."

"Yeah, ditto," I said. The moment I'd spoken I realized how rude it must have sounded. I got ready for an earful.

"Don't speak to me like that, Sarah. You can go

to Kelly's, but I want you back here by twelve-thirty. Got that?"

"That means I'll only be there for about an hour."

"That's right."

I went without saying 'bye, and as I was going out of the front door I heard Clemmie pipe up, "Does Sarah hate Steve like she hates Amanda?"

"No, she's just hasn't decided whether to like us or not yet," was the reply from Steve. He said it really casually as though Clemmie had asked him how tall he was.

All the way to Kelly's house I couldn't get it out of my head.

"Come in the back way," said Kelly, rushing out to meet me. "Mom and Dad are having a big row in the den, so I'm trying to keep away from them."

We crept in together and as we tiptoed upstairs

I could hear raised voices, only it sounded like three people.

"Tracy's in there too," explained Kelly in a whisper. (Tracy is Kelly's big sister.) "She wants to go to a night-club in Boston and Dad says she can't, and Mom thinks Dad's being too strict, but now the argument's grown and whatever anyone says, one of them goes crazy. I tell you, Sare, if I went in there and said, 'Sarah's here,' someone would turn on me and accuse me of telling lies," Kelly said, looking more than a little ticked off.

We'd only been in her room for about two minutes when the door was flung open so hard that it hit the wall.

"Can't you knock?" Kelly said sharply to her sister.

"Where are my new black pants?"

"How should I know?'

"Oh, come off it, Kelly. You're always taking my

things without asking, and I'm getting sick of it. Maybe I'll get a lock for my closet, then you'll have to wear your own clothes for a change."

"That is so unfair. I've never borrowed any black pants. I borrowed those grey ones a few times because you said you didn't like them any more. Apart from that, I only borrowed that new top last weekend, because it was a party. Anyway, I *did* ask you, it's just that you don't listen half the time."

"Look, Kelly, I'm going out and I need those black pants now, so just tell me where they are, will you?"

"I haven't a clue. How many more times – "

The door was slammed shut and we listened to furious footsteps banging their way downstairs. Because Kelly's room was directly above the kitchen, we then heard every word of another argument raging below. This one was between Tracy and her mother, and ended with

Tracy slamming out of the kitchen and banging the door of the den, hard.

After that, peace seemed to reign, apart from the noisy mower that Kelly's dad was pushing up and down the back lawn. Kelly and I decided to go down to the kitchen and raid the cookie jar. We'd no sooner got in there, than Kelly's mom marched in from the hall, looking like thunder. It was so funny when she caught sight of me and had to change her furious expression into a nice pleasant one for unexpected visitors.

"Hello, Sarah. All right?"

"Yes, thank you."

"That's good. Your mom all right?"

"Yes, thank you."

"Lucky her!"

She rolled her eyes, but it wasn't in a joking way.

"Here we go again," said Kelly, as soon as her mother had gone out of the back door into the garden.

We watched her go chasing after Kelly's dad, then start striding along beside him, as he pushed the shuddering great mower up and down. We could hear their screeching voices above the dreadful racket of the mower, but even if we hadn't been able to hear, anyone could see from their body language that they were arguing.

"Let's go into the other room," said Kelly.

So we did, only to find Tracy and Adam, Kelly's twelve-year-old brother, in the middle of yet another fight. From what I gathered, Tracy had told their parents that Adam had borrowed her cell phone and lost it, only Adam hadn't lost it. He'd lent it to a friend, who was going to bring it back at four o'clock.

"Well, you do *not* go lending my private property to your friends," said Tracy, rounding on Adam. "I have to go out right now! Four o'clock's too late. Phone your friend and tell him to get it here, pronto! And another thing – you realize I'll never ever lend you my phone again, don't you?"

"Good," said Adam. "And next time you forget your key and get home late, don't bother to chuck stones at my bedroom window because I won't come down and let you in."

"I see!" said Kelly's mom, storming into the den at that moment. "So, that's what you do, is it? Wake your brother up behind our backs?"

"Oh great! Thanks very much, Adam Big Mouth Jackson," retorted Tracy. I could see a vein sticking out in her neck and her cheeks were all red.

"Have you got any make-up on?" asked Adam.

"What's that supposed to mean?" Tracy came back at him, spitting in her fury.

"It's supposed to mean that you look really ugly – you know, uglier than usual," said Adam.

"Shut up, both of you," shouted Kelly, blocking her ears. "You might not have noticed, but I have actually got a visitor here, you know."

"Don't shout like that," said her mom. "You're getting very loud these days, Kelly."

"I have to be loud to make myself heard above all the arguing," Kelly replied in an even louder shout.

"Don't be so cheeky," said her mom.

"I wasn't being cheeky. I was just stating a fact," said Kelly.

I suddenly felt exhausted with all the noise and the fighting. Thank goodness it wasn't like this in my house.

The thought, when it came, hit me like a ton of bricks. I'd come to Kelly's house to get away from my own house, and yet right now, my own house seemed like a beautiful haven of peace and tranquility, even with Steve in it.

13. STEAK, FRIES AND PROFITEROLES

I looked at my watch in a very obvious way.

"Twelve-thirty! Oh no! I'd better hurry. I'm supposed to be home by now. We're going out to lunch for my birthday."

"Yes, Kelly said you'd just had your birthday. Well, have a lovely time, dear. Hope to see you another day."

"Thank you for having me, Mrs. Jackson."

"Pleasure, dear. Didn't even notice you were here, you're so quiet."

I half walked and half ran home, then pushed

open the back door, practically falling into the kitchen. Mom was taking washing out of the drier, humming to herself. Clemmie was drawing at the table. Her tongue was curled up over her top lip and she was making tiny grunting noises, which she always does when she's concentrating.

"Hi," said Mom, quietly.

"Hi," I replied, just as quietly.

The sound of our two gentle voices gave me a nice contented feeling, and without really thinking, I found myself apologizing for being late. As soon as I'd spoken I wondered what had come over me, because before I'd left, I'd been so mad with everyone, especially Steve. It suddenly seemed odd, the way I'd reacted. What had I found so bad about the helicopter and the grasshoppers? I felt a stab of guilt about my hostility towards Steve, and now he wasn't even here. No wonder! He probably didn't want to have lunch with a horrible girl who so obviously didn't like him. Clemmie must have read my mind.

"Steve's gone to get something," she said in a matter-of-fact voice. "We're meeting him in the rest-ront, OK?"

"Fine," I said.

And fine I felt. Everything felt fine in this quiet place, compared to the war zone I'd been in for the past hour.

Mom came and put her arms round me. "We're going to Racklins. Thought that would be your choice. Yes?"

I nodded and hugged her tight.

As we walked into the restaurant, the memory of that last birthday meal came flooding back to me. I felt so much more comfortable this time. True, Steve hadn't turned up yet so there was plenty of room for things to go wrong, but somehow I doubted they would, because it didn't seem to matter what was happening around me. The inside of me was peaceful now so everything else was less important.

We sat down and I suddenly remembered the joke that *she* had told us. *What goes black, white, black, white, black, white?* I never did find out what the punchline was. Too bad. If it had been funny I could have told everyone over dessert.

It was as we were studying the menu that Steve came in.

"Hi," he said, pulling a small but bulky envelope out of his pocket and plonking it on the table by Mom's side plate.

Mom whipped it into her handbag without a word. You didn't have to be the most sensitive person in the world to work out that this might well be my birthday present. Clemmie's eyes were wide, and I could tell she was bursting to speak, but Mom was fixing her with a stern frown, so she kept her mouth shut and stared at the menu. After a bit she started to go cross-eyed. I wasn't too sure if she was doing it because she was under strict instructions to keep something secret from me, or whether it was just one of Clemmie's strange facial experiments, but either way it was so funny, I couldn't help bursting out laughing.

The moment I cracked up, so did Steve. He let out a great guffaw of laughter and Mom gripped his arm and said, "Ssh! You'll get us all chucked out." But Steve couldn't stop laughing. He was like a little boy who'd been told off for giggling, but he simply couldn't help it, and the more he was supposed to stop, the more he couldn't.

"Sorry," he spluttered. "It's just that Clemmie's so subtle."

Well, that made me crack up all over again.

"Sarah, you're as bad as Steve," said Mom,

frowning hard at me. "Try to control yourselves, you two."

Mom sat up straight like a very old-fashioned school teacher, and studied the menu with her head tipped on one side and a very prissy smile on her face. I think she was just trying to make up for me and Steve, who were still struggling to stop laughing, and Clemmie, who had sucked in her cheeks and made her lips into a strange sort of bow, her eyes still crossed.

"Can I take your order?" said the waitress.

"We're not quite ready just yet," said Mom, and the waitress said she'd be back in a minute.

"She'd better not be any longer than a minute or Clemmie will have turned into a goldfish," commented Steve.

I didn't know what was so highly amusing about that, but for some reason I just couldn't seem to stop laughing all the time.

The meal was amazing. I found I was starving,

and so did everyone else. I kept on wondering whether that bulky envelope that Steve had given to Mom was my birthday present and, if so, when Mom was going to give it to me. All through my steak and fries, whatever we were talking about, my mind kept wandering back to that envelope. Maybe she was planning on producing it with a flourish at the end of the meal. I ate my profiteroles at about a hundred miles per hour and then felt sick.

"I fink Sarah's been stuffing her face," commented Clemmie in a very motherly voice, which made Mom laugh.

"Well, you're allowed to eat fast when you're celebrating something," said Steve.

Surely Mom will give me the present now, I thought. When the coffee had come and gone, and the bill had been paid (Mom and Steve split it, I noticed), I decided that I must have been mistaken about the contents of that envelope.

I could hardly move I felt so full as we went out to the car park. Steve gave Mom a quick kiss and ruffled Clemmie's hair, saying, " 'Bye, little goldfish," then he turned to me.

"Thanks for letting me tag along, Sarah. I really enjoyed that."

I was taken aback. "Yeah, m-me too," I stammered.

"Is Steve coming back to our house?' asked Clemmie.

" 'Fraid I can't. Got to get back to the shop."

"What shop?"

"Steve's got the most wonderful smelling shop in the whole country," Mom explained. "He sells every kind of coffee bean that exists."

So *that's* what Mom and Dad had been joking about!

"Can you come to our house tomorrow, Steve?" asked Clemmie in a begging tone.

"Yes, that would be great," I found myself agreeing.

"That's an invitation I can't refuse," said Steve, "if your mom doesn't mind, that is."

Mom just smiled.

"Very early curly," added Clemmie.

"OK, I'll be knocking on the door at six o'clock in the morning. All right?"

"You dare!" said Mom.

It was odd, but I felt quite deflated. It had been such a great lunch, and I wished Steve could come back with us so the fun could carry on.

When we got home Mom told me to sit down, then she brought out the bulky envelope that Steve had given her, opened it, and there was my present, all wrapped up in purple and yellow paper.

"Happy birthday, dear," she said.

On the front it said TO SARAH WITH ALL MY

LOVE FROM MOM.

I peeled off the wrapping and gasped when I saw my present. It was a cell phone!

"Awesome!" I breathed. "Oh, thank you very very much! I never thought I'd get one of these."

"Glad you're pleased," said Mom with a sort of sheepish smile.

"How come Steve brought it to the restaurant, Mom?" I asked her.

"Because he's only just bought one for his son, so he knew exactly what he was asking for. I really didn't have a clue, because there's so much choice around. So Steve offered to get yours for me, but he wasn't free to pick it up till this morning."

"Why isn't it from Steve and Mommy?" asked Clemmie, with her nose about an inch away from the wrapping paper, as though the name Steve might suddenly spring before her eyes if she studied it closely enough.

"Because we don't know Steve well enough for

that yet," Mom replied.

"Oh yes, and we've got to wait to see if Sarah likes him, haven't we?"

I blushed.

Clemmie's voice dropped to a whisper.

"Do you like him, Sarah?"

"Don't be so nosy," said Mom, tapping the end of Clemmie's nose. I knew she was only trying to get me out of having to answer an embarrassing question.

"Yes, I do," I replied without hesitation.

Mom didn't look at me. She went over to the drier and picked up the basket of clothes that she'd got out earlier on. When she looked up I saw a lovely smile covering her face. She was humming again as she went out of the kitchen.

14. MEETING JACK FOWLER

"Lauren, are you trying to send me on some kind of guilt trip or something?'

"No, I'm just trying to be your friend." We were sitting in Rollins at half-past four on Monday. This was our favourite place. A lot of kids from our school came in here, on Saturdays mainly. "What's the difference between Steve and Amanda?"

"The difference is that I hate *her* because she took Dad away from our perfectly happy family and now she's acting like she's my mother, trying to control everything. And I just hate her."

"Maybe it wasn't a perfectly happy family before."

"It *was*," I snapped. Lauren opened her mouth to speak but then shut it again. "Go on," I went on more calmly. "What were you going to say?"

"I was going to ask if you wanted another éclair, but then I remembered that you didn't have one in the first place."

When I got home, Mom said that Dad had called to speak to me, and he'd call back later.

"What, he called me from work?"

"I suppose so."

My mind went into overdrive. He must have wanted to talk to me privately – away from *her* ears. It was probably only building castles in the air but I couldn't help hoping he was planning on leaving her.

The next time the phone rang, I ran to answer

it, but it wasn't Dad. It was Steve. I told him how great I thought my cell phone was, and he asked me for the number and said he'd phone me one day. Then he chatted with Mom for ages.

About an hour later Dad rang. He mentioned something funny that had happened at work and then he asked about my weekend. I decided that it might be a bit tactless to mention that we'd been out for a meal with Steve, but it was rather awkward when he asked me if I was pleased with my present from Mom.

"Er . . . yes, it was great," I replied hesitantly.

"Good. I thought you'd like it."

"You mean, you know what it is?"

"Yes. Mom told us beforehand what she was getting you. Amanda and I have got a note of your number. You never know when we might need it!"

He laughed, and I tried to laugh too, but it wasn't easy. I was thinking back to what *she'd* said in the restaurant on my birthday. Had she just made something up on the spur of the moment to put me off the scent of Mom getting me the phone? Was all that stuff about how I had to be the same age as Frankie just a smokescreen? Dad's next words jolted me back to the present.

"Anyway, Sarah, I'm just calling about Saturday afternoon . . ."

I tensed up, wondering what he was going to say. I'd no idea whether he'd decided to go ahead with the outing or to cancel it to teach me a lesson. It was strange, but ever since I'd realized that the whole thing might be off, I'd felt more and more like going.

"I hope you're all geared up for it?" Dad said.

I breathed out.

"Yes, I'm really looking forward to it."

"Good. I know you're going to love it. I'll pick you up on Friday at six-thirty."

There was something I had to know.

"Who exactly is going to whatever it is on Saturday?"

"All of us," he replied firmly.

I didn't say anything, but disappointment was seeping into my spirits like fine drizzle. Dad obviously sensed that I wasn't exactly over the moon. His voice was full of that false brightness again.

"See you on Friday then."

I muttered something that passed for "All right. See you."

At school a few days later, I was in the corridor waiting for Lauren to come out of her Spanish class when a boy's voice behind me made me jump.

"Are you Sarah Dale?"

I turned to see a tall dark boy. He must've been in eleventh grade at least, and it was unusual for people out of your grade to talk to you, especially boys.

"Yeah."

"You know my dad then?"

"Er . . . no."

"I'm Jack Fowler." Still I must have looked blank. "My dad's Steve."

I frowned and then my eyes shot open wide, as I made the connection.

"Oh, right . . . Hi."

His mouth turned up at the corners but I can't say that it was a proper smile.

"How was lunch at Racklins?"

"It was good. I mean, great. It was for my . . . birthday."

"So I gather. Happy Birthday, by the way."

"It was last Thursday."

"Happy Birthday for last Thursday then. Seeya."

And he went, leaving me feeling guilty and a bit shaky. I wished I could sit down.

For the rest of the day, I couldn't stop thinking about Jack Fowler. I wondered how he felt about his dad going out to lunch with Mom and me. And I wondered why I didn't resent Steve the way I did *her*. I decided it was because Steve didn't act like *she* did. He didn't try to be my parent. He hadn't even tried to muscle in on my birthday present.

I'd convinced myself that there was nothing at all for me to feel guilty about, so why did I still feel guilty?

When I got home Mom said that Dad had phoned. Mom was to tell me that *she* was very sorry but she wouldn't be able to come on the birthday outing after all, because her mother was ill and she had to go and visit her on Friday after work. She wouldn't be back until Sunday evening.

"Oh, right," I said, wondering why I wasn't feeling happier. After all, this was exactly what I wanted to happen. Wasn't it? So what was it that was dragging my spirits in the direction of my shoes?

15. REWIND

On Friday evening at six-thirty on the dot, Dad came to the door. Clemmie flung it open and lugged him in to look at her picture of a grasshopper. Mom offered Dad a cup of tea and he accepted. He even stayed for a second one. They chatted away like old friends. When Dad eventually made a move to go, I couldn't help noticing the sympathetic smiles that he and Mom exchanged.

It seemed strange going into a dark house. It was

so quiet. Clemmie wanted to know when Frankie and Charlie would be back. Dad said they'd been invited to a last-minute party and were sleeping over.

"I'll make dinner, OK?" he went on. He was trying to be cheery, but it wasn't coming off. It suddenly struck me that he was probably missing *her*. "Clemmie, you come and choose which pasta you want, while Sarah takes the bags upstairs. Decide which bedroom you want, Sarah, and put Clemmie in the other one," he added.

My footsteps were heavy on the stairs. At the top I pushed open the door of the room where we'd all four slept the last time. I'd been expecting it to look like it did before, with sleeping bags on the floor, so it came as a shock to see just one bed. The room looked bigger and tidier. I was puzzled though, because I thought the girls shared a bedroom. I went across the landing and looked in the bedroom where Mark had slept the last time. There was just one bed in here too, but this wasn't the spare room. It was clearly Charlie's room. It even said *CHARLIE'S ROOM* on the door.

I sat down heavily on the bed. They must have just pretended that they shared a room so that Mark wouldn't feel bad about kicking Charlie out of her room, and we wouldn't feel bad about invading Frankie's room. I left Clemmie's bag in Charlie's room and went back into Frankie's. It felt wrong to be in Frankie's bedroom when she wasn't there. I wondered if they'd really been invited to a party or whether they'd remembered the last time I came to stay, and thought they'd rather not go through that again. I didn't blame them. I'd acted terribly.

A picture of Jack Fowler flashed through my mind. Did he feel about me how I felt about Frankie and Charlie? No, he couldn't. There was nothing to hate about me . . . I looked at the smiling faces of Frankie and Charlie in the photo, and it hit me in a flash. There was actually nothing to hate about them either. But wait a minute . . . I'd smashed this photo and yet here it was, good as new.

Something caught my eye beside it. An envelope with my name on the front was propped up against the mirror on the dressing table. I opened it.

"Hi Sarah,
So sorry not to be able to come tomorrow. I hope you have a wonderful time. Can you feed Rosie for me (night and morning), please? You know where all the stuff is. Your dad is very forgetful about that kind of thing! If you're still here on Sunday at about 5, I'll see you then. Otherwise it'll be in a couple weeks.
Love, Amanda."

My throat hurt and I felt another stab of guilt as I put the letter in my bag.

I rushed down to see Rosie, feeling pleased that I'd been given the job of feeding her. Until that moment I'd forgotten all about the poor dog.

That evening was strange. Dad, Clemmie and I played cards, watched television, ate dinner, talked. But nothing felt right. Clemmie had a bath and went to bed. I played a few card tricks on Dad but they didn't seem that good. I couldn't concentrate because pictures kept flashing through my mind – Jack Fowler, then Charlie, Frankie and *her*. The guilt I felt was becoming too much to bear.

The next morning I was up early. I fed Rosie and took her for a walk.

"What time are the girls going to be home?" I asked Dad.

"About eleven. And we're going out to you-know-where at one-thirty."

As the morning wore on I felt my spirits rising. It was funny, I was actually looking forward to Frankie and Charlie coming back. This house wasn't right with just me and Dad and Clemmie in it.

When they came rushing in I had a moment of panic in case everything went wrong again. They stopped in mid-rush and eyed me warily for a second, as though I was a wild animal and might scratch them to pieces at any moment. It was no wonder really. They must have hated me and yet here they were, all wariness instantly replaced by friendly smiles.

"Hi," I said. "I'm glad you're back. It felt really strange here without you."

There was a moment's silence, as though the girls couldn't believe that I was acting like a human being. Then they both started chatting away and led me and Clemmie upstairs, tossing a couple of "Hi, Robert's" over their shoulders.

When we got to the top of the stairs, Charlie ran down again, gave Dad a kiss then raced back up. I laughed, because Dad looked so astonished.

"It's getting pretty boring down here," Dad called up about half an hour later, when the four of us were in the middle of a really silly game of "Twister".

"Coming in a minute, you handsome old prince," called Clemmie, which made us all crack up.

Just before we went back down I wanted to find something out.

"This is a good photo," I said casually to Frankie, as I pointed to the one that I'd broken.

"Yeah. It's the only one we've got of all four of us. Sue – that's our dad's new wife – came round to collect us one time, and she took that picture. Mom said she was polishing last week and she broke it – clumsy thing. Anyway, it has a new frame now. Come on, let's go down and see your dad. You're so lucky having such a cool dad. Only two hours to lift-off!"

She raised her right hand and I raised mine, then we high fived. Half of me was so happy that history wasn't repeating itself. I'd shaken off so much of my jealousy and anxiety. But the other half felt terrible. *She* must have realized exactly how the photo had got smashed, and she'd taken the blame on herself. How stupid I'd been to hate her without even knowing her!

Charlie and Clemmie had disappeared downstairs and Frankie was on her way.

"Just going to the washroom," I said.

As soon as I heard the door to the kitchen close I crept into *her* and Dad's room. The phone, as I guessed it would be, was by their bed. On the back was their personal directory of stored numbers. The first one was *Peter* (her ex-husband), the second was *Mother*. After that were a couple of names I'd never heard of, and then I saw *Debra* (that's Mom). With a shaking hand I pressed the talk button followed by memory 2 – *her* mother. My heart was beating wildly as four rings sounded, and then an over-whelming disappointment hit me when I heard the answering machine message. I cleared my throat.

"I'm sorry to disturb you, but if . . . *Amanda*" (there, I'd said it) "is with you, I was wondering if you could say that Sarah called, and we'll be going on the outing soon, and I was wondering if . . . I mean, I really wish she could come too . . ." The machine cut out at that point. I must have hesitated too long.

I put the phone down, feeling completely stupid. I'd never left such a ridiculous message on an answering machine before. I bet Amanda wasn't even there. She'd probably gone to stay with a friend, so she could pour out her problems about her partner's hateful daughter. If only I could rewind fifteen days and start all over again!

We drove to the rec center and went inside. I was completely baffled. What on earth were we going to see? Frankie stayed glued to my side, and Charlie held Clemmie's hand, which left Dad all on his own. Poor Dad! If I hadn't been so selfish he'd have Amanda with him now. What a lot they'd put up with to try and keep me happy! A conversation from exactly a week before flashed into my head.

"Does Sarah hate Steve likes she hates Amanda?"

"No, she's just not decided whether or not to like us yet."

He was right. I hadn't. But I thought I had now.

A massive poster was facing me. It said MAGIC in big letters, and then in even bigger letters, DALE CLYDE. I couldn't believe my eyes! Dale

Clyde is the biggest name in magic at the moment. I'd often seen him on television. And today he was right here in this very building where I was standing. Even better, I was just about to see him. Awesome! I loved magic shows: conjurors, illusionists, escapologists — every type of magician. But Dale Clyde was the best.

I turned to look at Dad. He was smiling at me. No wonder, I must have been quite a funny sight with my mouth hanging open.

"What a great idea!" I told him, slipping my hand through his arm.

"Glad you're impressed."

The girl on the door to the theater hall said, "Only five of you, sir?" to Dad.

Dad looked a bit embarrassed because he'd handed over six tickets. I felt the biggest stab of guilt I'd felt yet. And the guilt turned to sadness when we sat down — Charlie, Clemmie, Frankie,

Dad, me. And beside me an empty seat.

I sat there with a lump in my throat, letting everyone's chatter wash over me. Any minute now the lights would go down and the show would begin. Poor Amanda! It looked as though she'd stayed away to make sure I would come. It had to be that. After all, she'd been proved right on that fateful evening of my birthday. And now Dad didn't have his partner at his side, and Charlie and Frankie didn't have their mother.

"Do you want some popcorn, Dad?" asked Clemmie, leaning over Frankie.

But Dad was craning round in his seat. His face was suddenly covered with a look of disbelief. I knew, before I followed his gaze, who I was going to see. An enormous cloud lifted off me. At the back of the hall, scanning the masses of seats in front of her, was Amanda. She'd had her hair cut very short. It made her look younger.

I liked it short. I hoped she would keep it like that. It suited her.

She saw Dad first and bit her lip. Then her eyes settled on mine and she smiled nervously. I leapt out of my seat and rushed over to her.

"Did you get my message? I didn't really say it properly. I meant – "

"Yeah, I got it. Did you get mine?"

I looked blankly at her.

"I sent you a text message."

I'd forgotten all about my cell. I pulled it out of my pocket and pressed the buttons. And there was Amanda's message: *I'm on my way. Love, Amanda.*

"I wish I'd checked. I've been sitting here, dying for you to come."

"Bet I know why." I looked at her, not understanding. "You wanted to know the punchline to that joke, *What goes black, white, black, white, black, white?* didn't you?"

I waited.

"A nun falling down the stairs."

It wasn't really funny, but for me it was the most hilarious joke I'd ever heard. We laughed as we went down to our seats. Amanda gave Dad a quick kiss, whispered something to him which made him smile at me, then came and sat in the spare seat beside me. Frankie, Charlie and Clemmie looked utterly astounded. Happy, but astounded. The lights started to dim just as my cell phone vibrated. I only just managed to read the message in the poor light.

"Hope the treat is going well. See you soon. Love, Steve."

"It's from Mom's boyfriend," I whispered in the dark to Amanda. "He says he hopes the treat's going well. I'll phone him afterwards."

"What will you say?"

"It's the best treat of my life."

"Mine too," she whispered.

And then it was completely dark, but inside me
a thousand bright candles burned.

What happens next in the step-chain?
Meet Ollie in

YOU CAN'T FALL FOR YOUR STEP-SISTER

1. THE COUNTDOWN

My name's Oliver Banks. That's the longest version, strictly reserved for teachers – *"Oliver Banks, I don't appear to have received your homework."* Then there's Oliver, which is what Mom calls me when she's not happy. But my friends all call me Ollie.

I live with my mom and my stepdad, Peter. He's really cool. He jokes around a lot and isn't as strict as my real dad. Not that I like my real dad any less than Peter. It's just that he's not so laid back.

Right now it's summer vacation and I'm counting down the days till we go away for a couple weeks in New Jersey. Only three to go. I *think* I'm looking forward to it, but I'm not totally sure. The people going from my family are me, my mom, Peter and my brother Rory.

Fine so far. But . . . get this! Peter wants to bring his two daughters along. They don't live with us. They live with their mom, but come here to visit their dad (Peter) quite often. They're called Frankie and Charlie. I'm usually at my dad's when they come here, so I don't really get to see them all that much. Once or twice Charlie's been here on her own, and she seems OK, mucking about with Rory in the back yard or on his precious computer.

But going on holiday together — that's different. I bet Frankie and Charlie don't want to go away with two boys, any more than I want to go away with two girls.

"Oliver?"

Uh-oh! Mom didn't sound too happy.

"Yeah?" I answered, opening my bedroom door.

"How many times have I got to tell you to take your sneakers off at the back door?" she called up the stairs.

"But I came in at the front. With Peter."

"I realize that. There's a trail of muddy footprints going through the hall and all the way upstairs. I presume they go right into your bedroom. Come to the top of the stairs. Let me look at you."

I quickly took the sneakers off without undoing the laces, then went to the top of the stairs.

"Oh, Ollie. What am I going to do with you?"

"What's wrong? I've taken my trainers off."

"But your trackpants and your shirt are absolutely filthy! Do your friends go home looking as though they've been having a mud bath?"

Mom was exaggerating and she knew it. "You can't help getting dirty if you're playing football, Mom. Peter didn't tell me off," I couldn't resist adding.

"Peter probably didn't even notice. Anyway, I'm not arguing about it. Go and have a bath and by the time you've done that, dinner will be ready."

And that was when I remembered that I was supposed to be taking a video back to Sam Cotteril's. I'd promised I'd definitely do it today, because it belongs to his much older brother, who's going ape because I keep forgetting to give it back.

The trouble was, knowing Mom, there was no chance she'd let me go to Sam's even if I got down on my bended knee and begged. So there was only one thing to do.

I ran the bath water at top force, then turned the taps off, shut the bathroom door, and snuck downstairs and out the front door with the video. I got to Sam's in a record seven minutes.

"Hiya, Ollie. You look winded," he said, opening the door. "You can't be very fit. You should get yourself in training."

He grinned because everyone knows that Sam is the least fit person in the universe.

"Cut out the chat, Sam. I'm supposed to be in the bath. I'm risking another big blow-up from Mom, bringing this back for you."

"Bet you'd like to have a quick go on my new computer game though," he said, grinning even more and opening the door wider. "It only takes a few minutes and it's awesome, I can tell you."

I knew I should have just said no. Sam must have seen the hesitation on my face. (He could hardly have missed it — I was biting my lip and screwing my eyes up trying not to give in to temptation.)

"The thing is, Ollie," said Sam, yanking me in through the front door, "if you go home right away your body won't have had time to recover, but if you just rest for a few minutes you'll get back much faster, honest."

It seemed to make sense.

"OK. Only a few minutes though."

Sam's mom called out when Sam and I were practically at the top of the stairs. She's scary, Sam's mom. Her voice sounds too loud for the room. You're not supposed to use the word fat, so let's just say she's quite large and she always wears big swirly dresses, in bright colors like orange. Her hair's weird too. Sort of speckled blondish gray and shiny.

"Is that Oliver Banks, by any chance?" she boomed up the stairs. I turned around and gave her a shaky smile.

"Hello, Mrs. Cotteril." I've never had the guts to call her Pammy, which is what she likes people to call her. It just sounds stupid.

"I'm glad you're here, Oliver, because Samson — " I tried not to smirk " — tells me that your family is off to New Jersey in a few days' time, too. Such a coincidence!"

The bangles on her arm started jangling, like she needed a fanfare to go with her loud voice. I made a noise that was supposed to show that I agreed about the coincidence but didn't really want to talk about it any more.

"Ollie's only got a minute, Mom," said Sam, going up the last two stairs. I was about to follow when . . .

"Are you going anywhere near Ashbury Park on your travels, by any chance, Oliver?" Mrs. C's big voice rang up the stairwell.

"Um . . . I'm not sure —"

"What's the name of the place where you're staying? Hmm?"

"Um . . . Atlantic City."

She clapped her hands together and the clap echoed all the way up the stairs.

"Incredible! Such a coincidence! It's scarcely a stone's throw from Ashbury Park. Marvelous news. I will telephone your mother straight away and arrange a little get-together. We're staying with my sister and her daughter. Samson wasn't too sure that he wanted to spend a week in all-female company, were you, Samson?"

I whacked Sam's leg as subtly as I could to get him to stop his mom from phoning my mom. That would be just great, wouldn't it, when I was supposed to be in the bath? Sam must have thought I was trying to get away so we could play the computer game, because he turned and headed for his bedroom. His mom was still banging on in her foghorn voice, "But now you know Oliver is going to be around, I think we might detect a bit of an improvement in your attitude, hmm?"

"Um . . . actually, Mrs. Cotteril, Mom's out at the moment. I'll tell her to call you when she gets back."

"All right, Oliver. Thank you, dear."

And she went off singing in a high warbly voice in a foreign language. Poor Sam! I was glad my mom was quite an ordinary sort of mother so my friends couldn't make fun of me. It'd be good if he was near us on holiday though. But something told me Mom wasn't going to be too pleased. I don't think she's ever liked Mrs. Cotteril all that much.

It was beginning to look like coming to Sam's was one big mistake.

Collect the links in the step-chain . . .

2. Ollie thinks a holiday with girls will be a nightmare. And it is, because he's fallen for his stepsister. Can it get any worse? Find out in *You Can't Fall For Your Stepsister*

3. Lissie's half-sister is a spoiled brat, but her mom thinks she's adorable. Can Lissie make her see what's really going on? Find out in *She's No Angel*

4. Becca's mom describes her boyfriend's daughter as perfect in every way. Can Becca bear to meet her? Find out in *Too Good To Be True*

5. Ed's stepsisters are getting seriously on his nerves. Should he go and live with his mom? Find out in *Get Me Out Of Here*

6. Hannah and Rachel are stepsisters. They're also best friends. What will happen to them if their parents split up? Find out in *Parents Behaving Badly*